Discord

Millicent Min, Girl Genius

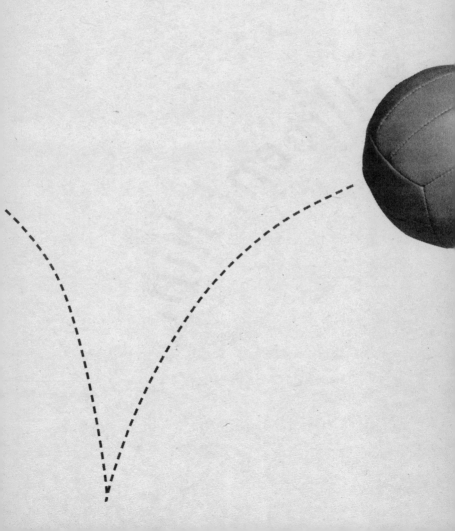

SCHOLASTIC INC.

New York Toronto London Auckland Sydney
Mexico City New Delhi Hong Kong Buenos Aires

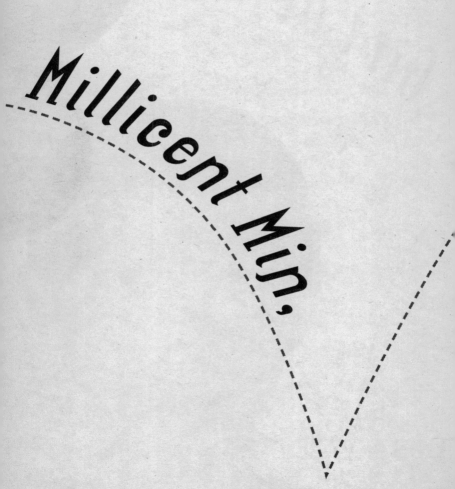

Millicent Min,

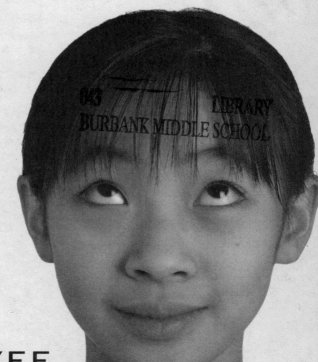

Girl Genius

by
LISA YEE

Text copyright © 2003 by Lisa Yee.
All rights reserved. Published by Scholastic Inc.
SCHOLASTIC, the LANTERN LOGO
and associated logos are trademarks and/or registered
trademarks of Scholastic Inc.

Arthur A. Levine Books hardcover edition designed by
Elizabeth Parisi, published by Arthur A. Levine Books,
an imprint of Scholastic Inc., October 2003

ISBN 0-439-42520-4

12 11 10 9 8 7 6 5 4 3 2 1   4 5 6 7 8 9/0

Printed in the U.S.A.   40

First paperback printing,
January 2004

This book is dedicated to my mother,
the smartest girl I know.
—L.Y.

Special thanks to . . .
Arthur for helping me find my voice
Cheryl for her devotion to Millie and Moon Pies
Benny and Kate for making every day a special one
And especially to Scott, for always believing in me

Millicent L. Min

521 Ridgeside Drive
Rancho Rosetta, CA 92219
MillicentMin@magicpencil.com

AGE: 11 and a half

IMMEDIATE OBJECTIVE(S): To become JFK High School valedictorian, win the National Math Bowl Championship, earn a scholarship to an Ivy League university of my choice

LONG-TERM OBJECTIVE(S): To be awarded the Fields Medal, MacArthur Grant, and other prestigious honors, and to embark on several careers including psychometrician, journalist, judge, and acclaimed pastry chef

EDUCATION:

AGE †	GRADE	SCHOOL
3	(Pre-K)	Mommy and Me Montessori
4	(K) and 1	Rancho Rosetta Elementary
5	2 and (3)	Rancho Rosetta Elementary
6	4	Rancho Rosetta Elementary and Star Brite
7	5	Star Brite
8	6 and (7)	Star Brite
9	8	Star Brite
10	9 and (10)	JFK High School
11	11	JFK High & Rogers College

† *at year-end*   ( ) *indicates grades skipped*

TELEVISION APPEARANCES: *The Tonight Show with Jay Leno* (age 2); affiliate news (ages 3, 5, and 9); Rancho·Rosetta public service commercial "Be Smart, Don't Litter" (age 4); PBS special "Bright Starts, Fast Starts — The Gifted Child" (age 7); *Jeopardy! for Kids* (age 8); *et cetera*

FEATURED IN NEWS ARTICLES: *TIME* ("The Genesis of Genius"); *Rancho Rosetta Examiner* ("Local Girl Outsmarts the System"); *Cryptarithm Lover's Journal* ("Min to the Max"); *Tomorrow's Child Today* ("How Smart Is Too Smart?"); *USA Today* ("Youngster Solves Levinklein Code"); *et cetera*

RECENT AWARDS: Math Bowl — first place (State), third place (Nationals); Global Warming essay — first place; Odyssey of the Mind — first place; National Science Search — finalist; Rancho Rosetta Library Read-a-Thon — first place (every year since age three); *et cetera*

JFK HIGH SCHOOL ACTIVITIES: Math Team (treasurer, team captain); Latin Club (treasurer); Honor Society (vice president); Dean's List (every semester); Chess Club; canned food drive co-coordinator; *Rocketeer* staff; *Nosh & Nib* — featured poem; hall monitor; *et cetera*

I have been accused of being anal retentive, an over-achiever, and a compulsive perfectionist, like those are bad things. My disposition probably has a lot to do with the fact that I am technically a genius. Unfortunately, this label seems to precede me wherever I go.

This afternoon I sped over to Maddie's house on my bike. I was anxious to escape the hysteria the last day of high school seems to inspire. Kids flinging their arms around each other. Teachers grinning with wild looks in their eyes. Yearbooks flying back and forth in an autographing frenzy.

As I emptied the contents of my locker into my briefcase earlier in the day, I had been optimistic that someone might ask me to sign their *Rocketeer*. In anticipation of this, I had drafted a truly original inscription — one that would showcase my sense of humor, something I have had little chance to share with my fellow students. I would start with *Quantum materiae materietur marmota monax si marmota monax materiam possit materiari?* Which, translated from Latin, means "How much wood would a woodchuck chuck if a woodchuck could chuck wood?" And then, here's the really funny part, I'd close with *Vah! Denuone Latine loquebar? Me ineptum. Interdum modo elabitur.* In English, that's "Oh! Was I speaking Latin again? Silly me. Sometimes it just sort of slips out." I would then finish with a flourish, "Signed, Millicent L. Min."

Eagerly, I waited for someone to stop long enough to hand me their *Rocketeer.* But the kids and their cliques just swarmed past without even slowing down. After a while it became clear I was not on the top (or even the bottom) of anyone's autograph list. So I wrote my Latin inscription in my own yearbook and then bid John F. Kennedy High good-bye until the next school year.

As I rounded the corner on my bike, I relaxed at the familiar sight of Maddie's house, a tidy white bungalow with green shutters and a bright red door. Despite the front-porch ceiling fan chugging away in a valiant effort to ward off the heat, my grandmother did not appear to be home. With nothing better to do, I camped out on the steps and reread my *Rocketeer.*

All the students look so much older than me. Yet that's to be expected. It's hard to believe I will be a senior next year. When I look back at my childhood, it doesn't seem like so long ago. Maddie swears it's because childhood is a state of mind. My mother insists that it's because I am only eleven years old. *Whatever.*

By the time Maddie arrived in her beat-up Dodge Dart, I had

found twenty-three typos in the yearbook. Four of those were misspellings of my name.

"Have you been here since school got out?" Maddie asked as she leapt out of the car. She doesn't act old, and no one has had the nerve to tell her she's a senior citizen. Without waiting for my reply, Maddie wrestled with a dragon in the backseat. It was about half my size and carved out of wood. "I can't believe you're still here," she said as she signaled for help. "School must have ended hours ago."

"Of course I'm still here," I told her as I held the car door open. I decided not to ask what the dragon was for. With Maddie, sometimes it's better not to know. "Where else would I be?"

Maddie smiled when she saw my *Rocketeer*. "How many times are you in it this year, Millie?" she asked.

"Twelve," I answered proudly.

"That's great. Did a lot of kids sign your yearbook?"

I don't really hang around with a lot of other students. I'm more of what you might call "an independent." Still, I did manage to get one, and almost two, autographs at lunch today.

Tommy Loescher is the Chess Club President and had prided himself on never having lost a match, until I joined the club. "Sure, I'll sign your yearbook, Millicent," Tommy said as a grin crossed his face. "Just let me finish my sandwich first."

His friends snickered as he chewed slowly. I wasn't sure what was so funny, but not wanting to appear rude, I laughed along with them. Then, wouldn't you know it, the bell rang before Tommy even had a chance to get out a pen.

"Oops," he said, popping what was left of his sandwich into his mouth, "gotta run! Sorry, Millicent. Maybe next year."

"But you're graduating . . ." I yelled as I watched him and his pals disappear into the crowd. Luckily, at that very moment Amy Drew crossed my path. Amy Drew is this year's valedictorian. I admire her immensely, and she has never failed to return my hellos in the hallway. Here is what she wrote:

Millie, stay cool!
Love always,
Amy D.

I spent my entire Honors English class analyzing her message. She could have been referring to the hot summer months Rancho Rosetta is famous for when she wrote "stay cool!" Or, and I like to think this is what she meant, Amy could have used the word "cool" as in "she's so cool." Thereby implying that I am one of the cool people, and that I should remain so.

Whatever her meaning, I am honored that Amy Drew signed my copy of the *Rocketeer*. I've already begun practicing my signature in anticipation of next year. Maybe when I'm valedictorian my autograph will be more sought after.

"Did you get any of the other students to sign your book?" Maddie pressed me again.

"Well . . . guess what?" I exclaimed. "I'll bet I am the only one lucky enough to get every teacher's signature!" My favorite was from Coach Frank. Despite his severe crew cut, he has a wild sense of humor. Coach had written:

> Millicent,
> You are the pride of our Math Bowl team. Can't wait to have you back next year when we sweep at Nationals!
>
> Coach Frank
> P.S. Why is 6 scared of 7? Because 7 — 8 — 9!!!

Maddie laughed when I read her Coach's joke. Then she put her arm around me. "C'mon Millie, it's time to get this dragon into the house and get some cold lemonade into us!"

As Maddie handed me my drink, I pulled out "Millicent's List of Splendid Summer Activities" from my briefcase. I've planned a lot of exciting adventures for Maddie and me. Since Grandpa died earlier this year, my grandmother's been depressed. So, to cheer her up I make sure I'm always around. She looked the list over, saying, "Hmm," as she read each entry, sometimes changing her response to "Ahhh" and "Uh-huh." I made sure to include projects I thought Maddie might enjoy, such as plotting the downtown traffic patterns or building a subterranean ant village.

Finally, Maddie placed her reading glasses on the top of her head. She already had two other pairs of glasses there, her driving glasses and her sunglasses.

"You know, Millie . . ." she said slowly. The ice clinked as she took a sip of lemonade. "I was thinking of maybe doing some things on my own this summer, like taking yoga. Maybe you should do some things on your own too. A young girl like you needs to branch out, find new friends her own age."

I considered how yoga involves emptying your mind, the complete opposite of what I strive to do. Noticing my frown, Maddie quickly added, "Of course, that doesn't mean we won't spend time together. Anyway, I thought that Monday was going to be the start of your new life. Isn't that what you've been telling me?" Her eyes twinkled mischievously.

Ah yes, Monday. That's when I will be attending my very first college class. It was Maddie who convinced my parents to let me go, though at first they insisted they needed to think about it.

"What's there to think about?" Maddie had asked. "The tea leaves say it's what she needs."

My grandmother often consults the tea leaves, and if they don't tell her what she wants, she simply moves them around until they do.

Mom and Dad pursed their lips as if they had just eaten some lemons. "Come on, Millie," Maddie sighed, taking my shoulders and facing me toward the door. "When their faces start scrunching up like that, it's our invitation to leave so they can talk about us."

"You didn't even begin to convince them," I complained as she marched me into the living room. "What am I supposed to do for the rest of my life? Hang around the house?"

"I planted the seed," she said. "Then I backed down when they were expecting a fight. They'll come around on their own. You'll see."

Sure enough, that night a Min Family Meeting had been called. At Min Family Meetings, problems/challenges/grievances are aired, discussed, and voted on. It is not as democratic as it may seem. My parents always have a secret Pre-Min Family Meeting first. They've read lots of parenting books that instruct them to prepare a unified front. What they don't know is that I've read the same books, so I know what to expect from them.

"Millie," my mother began solemnly. "College is a big step,

especially for someone who's only eleven." I held my breath and braced myself for the bad news. "Now, listen carefully," she said. "Here's the deal. . . ."

I could not believe it. . . . My parents actually agreed to let me take one college course! The caveat being that it had to be something "fun" and not have anything to do with numbers. Just because I once stayed awake for fifty-three hours straight to work out a complicated equation, Mom and Dad think I have an unhealthy obsession with math.

After much consideration, I have selected Professor Skylanski's Classic and Contemporary Poetry class. I'm looking forward to studying the great poets, interacting with my intellectual peers, and putting high school behind me — at least for the summer.

"Well, perhaps you'll make more friends in school next year," Maddie mused as she tried placing her dragon in various spots in the kitchen. "Then I'm sure your yearbook will be filled with autographs. Or maybe," she said nonchalantly, "you could befriend that nice boy, Stanford Wong. I hear he's having some problems in school."

I quickly changed the subject. Just thinking about stupid Stanford Wong is enough to creep me out. "I have plenty of friends," I assured Maddie. "Like Mrs. Martinez from the library. And what about Coach Frank? He's my friend."

Maddie just smiled. "You know," she said, "in China dragons

are considered good luck. You ought to have a dragon for your journey. One never knows where life might lead."

"We're not in China, we're in America," I pointed out. "Besides, I know exactly where I'm headed." It's true. I've mapped out my goals for the next fourteen years.

"Try veering off the road now and then," Maddie suggested as she lugged her dragon around the room. "Take a few side trips, see where you end up. You might be pleasantly surprised."

I stifled a laugh as I sipped my lemonade. Everyone knows that the shortest distance between two points is a straight line. Why would I want to take any other route?

I feel a duty to report that prior to this, my soon-to-be-triumphant debut at Rogers College, I have had, shall we say, some less successful summer endeavors.

Summer camp is no longer a possibility due to the unfortunate episode last year at Crystal Day Camp. Barbie, my counselor, felt compelled to call my parents to retrieve me after I threatened to sue. (I had found several health and safety violations.) And summer school at JFK High is not even an option. I've already completed so many classes that if I take any more, there won't be any left when I am a senior in the fall.

Everyone keeps making a fuss about my graduating next year. I can't wait. I want to get on with my life, go to college, embark on the first of several careers, and win the Fields Medal — the highest mathematical honor a person under forty can receive. It would be great to do all this by age twenty, but I don't want to put too much pressure on myself. Therefore, if it doesn't happen until I am, say, twenty-three, that's fine with me.

My age has always been an issue. Not for me, but for everyone else. Even starting at JFK was a big deal. I was nine at the time. On my first day of high school, my grandparents, parents, and the press insisted on tagging along. I made them walk four paces behind me, since I didn't want to stand out.

The next morning I was mortified to learn that the Associated Press picked up a photo of me on tippytoes trying to reach the top of my locker while a couple of basketball players stood by and gawked. The caption on the photo read "High school may not be a big stretch for nine-year-old Millicent Min, but her locker sure is."

In time things calmed down. Now new students stare, but most of the upperclassmen are used to me, and instead of being known as "that smart little girl," I am vilified as "the one who brings up the curve."

I had a difficult start, though. It's embarrassing enough being a foot shorter and five years younger than your peers, but then to have your grandmother cemented to you makes it even worse.

My parents allowed me to go to high school with the condition that during freshman year, Maddie would walk me to my first-period class. There, she was expected to hand me over directly to Gaspar, my habitually late French instructor whose real name was Lester. Maddie and I made an odd couple, but at least it meant I had somebody to talk to while the other kids made it a point to ignore me.

We were well into the first week and waiting outside Gaspar/Lester's class when someone, I never did figure out who, made an offending remark using the words "boring," "brainiac," and "Millicent" in the same run-on sentence. Believing I was being ridiculed, my grandmother warned my classmates that she knew kung fu and was not afraid to use it. To show how serious she was, Maddie did a series of complicated martial arts moves involving low blocks, high kicks, and several impressive jump spins.

There was a gasp from the crowd and immediately everyone backed away, fearing Maddie might hurt herself. When she was done and the applause petered out, Maddie was still in her age-defying leg-split position.

"Get up," I hissed. "Everyone's staring."

"No can do," she whispered. "I appear to be stuck."

By then Gaspar/Lester had arrived. He asked for volunteers and several of the bigger boys carried my grandmother to the school nurse's office as she waved adieu to first-period French.

"*Quel fromage*," murmured the girl next to me as we watched Maddie being carted away.

"*Dommage*," I said, smiling helpfully. "'*Quel fromage*' means 'which cheese.' '*Quel dommage*' means 'what a pity,' if that's what you meant to say."

Instead of saying thank you, the girl stared blankly at me like I was the one who was confused.

Luckily, Maddie will not be escorting me to college tomorrow. I'm looking forward to reinventing myself and forging new friendships. Friendships with students who are my peers, who use proper French vocabulary, and who won't think of me as just another dweeb in a toga. (But that's another story.)

This morning I was up before anyone else. I dressed, had breakfast (two s'mores Pop-Tarts, a banana, and a tall glass of chocolate milk) and was in the car honking the horn when my father stumbled into the garage. His hair was listing to one side like the Leaning Tower of Pisa and he was still in his pajamas, the ones with the dancing dogs and fire hydrants all over them.

"You're going like that?!?!" I asked, trying to mask my horror.

My father is fashion-impaired. Recently, he wore a Hawaiian shirt, albeit with his good pants, to an interview. (He did not get the job.) I myself was dressed in freshly laundered chinos, my best T-shirt, the one that says "Reality is merely an illusion," and, of course, white canvas Keds. As a vegetarian concerned about animal rights, I do not wear leather.

"Millicent, it's five-thirty in the morning. Your class does not begin until nine-thirty," Dad said, running his fingers through his hair and making it look worse, which was quite an achievement.

Well, duh. Of course I knew what time it was. I am never

without a watch, even when I sleep. It's just that I didn't want to be late. My mom and I have a thing about not being late. However, I must resort to desperate measures to ensure promptness, especially when waking up early is involved.

I am not a morning person, and I am suspicious of people who claim to be. It's just not natural. Therefore, I keep my alarm clock in my closet. That way, when it rings in the morning I am forced to get out of bed to shut it off. I also set my watch ahead by four minutes to fool myself into thinking I'm behind schedule. It's a strategy I learned from my mother. Our motto is "Better an hour early than a minute late." This morning, though, I was so excited about college that I couldn't sleep, thereby making waking up a foregone conclusion.

After much debate, my father and I came to a compromise. We left the house at 7:30 A.M., giving us ten minutes to get to college, ten minutes to find parking, twenty minutes to find my classroom, five minutes for him to get all mushy about "his little girl growing up," five minutes for me to get rid of him, ten minutes to organize my pens and paper, and an hour to wait for the professor.

I had a slight panic attack when the Honda stalled twice en route, once causing a minor traffic jam in front of Pep Boys. Luckily, I was able to make up the time since there was little need for me to organize my supplies, having pre-organized the night before.

Despite my traffic woes, I was the first person to arrive in class. I tried out several seats before settling on one in the front row, middle. Then I waited. By 9:25 I had almost passed out in anticipation. I had been dreaming about this moment for practically my whole life.

At 9:28 the door opened. I looked up, startled at the sight of someone balancing an overhead projector, a bonsai, *and* the biggest coffee mug I had ever seen. Professor Skylanski is everything I thought a college professor should be. She is smart and witty, and she dresses in a casual-chic way that seems thrown together, yet is immensely appropriate given the campus atmosphere. Even her glasses are professorial. We bonded instantly when we discovered we had the same briefcase.

"Who is that?" I heard someone whisper while Professor Skylanski and I were comparing organizers.

"A munchkin," another student snorted.

There are only ten people in our class. I would have thought there would be more since Classic and Contemporary Poetry is such an exciting subject. When Professor Skylanski surveyed the room, we found out that the other nine students are taking the class as a requirement and that I am the only one taking it for fun.

"W. B. Yeats, Emily Dickinson, Maya Angelou, this is all so wonderful!" I enthused. "I see where we cover all the major poets," I pointed out to Professor Skylanski. "But can we also squeeze in some minor ones, like Nicole Alexander or Ojo Kano? I know we only have class three days a week, but summer offers an ideal opportunity to concentrate on studies."

Upon hearing my suggestion, several students moaned until Professor Skylanski silenced them with a look worthy of my mother. She then informed everyone that the syllabus would remain as is, but anyone wishing additional work should stay after class. To my surprise, after we were dismissed I was the only student who stuck around.

I love being on campus. The great green expanse of lawn dotted with trees, the stately buildings, and especially the campus bookstore crammed with texts, school supplies, and every form of junk food imaginable. I cannot wait to attend college full-time.

Except for the apathy of the other students, my poetry class is everything I thought it would be. While I am eager to debate Professor Skylanski on the merits of iambic pentameter and the glorious nonsense of *Jabberwocky*, the rest of the room seems content to slouch and stare at the clock. It is their loss. That they appear to be fading into the bricks while I receive a private tutorial is fine with me.

Okay, so maybe I had imagined I would have endless discussions on politics and poetry with my peers, culminating in lively arguments and an exchange of footnotes. It is with dismay I've learned that the others in my class are more eager to talk about their weekend plans than Wordsworth's poems.

Therefore, it was with great delight that last Wednesday I made my first friend on campus. Her name is Debbie and she is a psychology major. I met her at the library. (The college library has more than twenty times more books than our local public branch.)

"Excuse me," she said as we reached for *Pride and Prejudice* at the same time. "Did you want this book too?"

"No, by all means go ahead," I told her. "I've already read it. I was just going to read it again for fun."

Her eyes widened. "Um, you've read this book?" she asked. I nodded. "My name's Debbie," she said, looking around. "Are you here waiting for someone?"

As I explained that I was officially enrolled in Rogers College and taking Classic and Contemporary Poetry over the summer, Debbie listened with rapt interest.

"Wow," she said. "That's so cool that you're so smart. I was supposed to read *Pride and Prejudice*, and this book too." She held up *The Psychology of Siblings*. "I've got a paper due in two days, and I haven't even started either book. Man, am I in trouble!"

"Oh!" I exclaimed. "I've read *The Psychology of Siblings*. It's fascinating." Debbie's jaw dropped. "I don't have any siblings," I explained. "But that doesn't mean I'm not interested in them."

"Say," she said, pushing her curly brown hair off her face and brightening considerably. "Can I buy you a milk shake or something? Maybe we could talk about these books."

"Sure!" I was so thrilled. Here it was, only my first week on campus and already I was hanging out with another college student. "I've got the whole afternoon open."

So that's how it started. Debbie loves to talk about her psychology class. She even lets me borrow her textbooks. Debbie considers me a confidante, and I am eager to share my insights with her. Today we met at the cafeteria, and she emoted about this guy Craig who doesn't appreciate her.

I enjoy listening to Debbie and feel grown up when we are together. Our relationship is going so well that in a totally reckless moment, I ordered a decaf coffee with cream and sugar. (How can anything that smells so good taste so bad?) As I pretended to sip my coffee, I gave her my unbiased opinion on the Craig situation.

"Gee, Millie, passive-aggressive behavior with undertones of narcissism?" Debbie echoed. "I just thought he was immature." Then she got so upset that she couldn't finish her chocolate mousse and she gave it to me.

We are having so much fun. I hope they never get back together.

When I suggested we take turns reading from my poetry book, Debbie suddenly remembered an important errand she had to run. Maddie had a hair appointment (she's promised not to dye it any more unnatural colors), so, with no place else to go, I packed up my briefcase and headed home.

Our house is small. "Cozy," my mother likes to say. It has a small patch of yard my dad has been "meaning to get to," a shower that mostly works, and a washer and dryer in my bedroom, since the only other alternative would be the front porch. Consequently, when I want to be alone I am forced to retreat to my tree.

My grandmother has a kinship toward trees and claims to have passed it on to me. There's a huge tree near the post office that's nicknamed the Lee Tree after my grandparents. It's a *Ficus benghalensis*, otherwise known as a banyan tree. In India they are considered sacred. When my mother was my age, my grandparents chained themselves to the tree to prevent it from being cut down and paved over. Now it's a local landmark and the road winds around it.

"Sometimes you have to work outside the system to effect change," Maddie says.

Mom still cringes every time we drive past it. "You don't know what it's like to have parents who embarrass you," she confides.

I always take the Fifth.

My tree is a big oak in the backyard. Technically, it belongs to the neighbors, but it branches out over our house. The Sponslers say they don't mind that I use it, as long as I continue to help them at tax time and promise not to fall out of the tree like I did once when I was five.

This afternoon, I climbed up my deciduous friend and settled into the natural crook that forms a perfect reading chair. My oak has a substantial trunk, and my fingertips barely touch when I put my arms around it. Dad designed a series of shelves that are held up by the branches without the benefit of nails. Here, I keep a legal pad, a good supply of black ballpoint pens (medium tip), and camouflage binoculars.

Perched in my tree with Debbie's psychology books, I surveyed the neighborhood. I could see Max, my little neighbor from down the street, smearing grape jelly all over his father's new white two-seater sports car. When his dad came storming out of the house, Max shrieked and threw the jelly jar over the fence. As I watched them run circles around the car, I marveled at how well my summer was progressing. A wonderful college class, a great friend, and access to thousands of books at the campus library. Nothing could dampen my spirits.

Oh. My. God. My life is over. My mother has signed me up for team sports. Why does she hate me so much? Is she exacting revenge because I put her through thirty-six hours of labor before her C-section?

I should report that Mom is athletic. Reedlike and quick, she was an alternate on the U.S. Women's Fencing Team. This contrasts with my father's laid-back style. He likes to do one thing at a time and takes great pride on his ability to focus. Mom insists focusing is an excuse Dad uses when he wants to ignore her.

Recently, Dad accused Mom of shrinking his pants. "It's not that your pants are shrinking," she parried. "But your waistline is expanding." Then this morning, my mother announces that our lack of organized physical activity is a detriment to our health and "something ought to be done about it."

While I appreciate the intellectual strategies some games involve, slogging up and down a designated area, sweating and grunting, is not my idea of a pleasant way to while away an afternoon. Therefore, imagine my discomfort when I heard Mom signed me up for the Rancho Rosetta Girls Summer Volleyball League. In four short days, my carefree summer will cease and volleyball will commence. No amount of debate could change my mother's mind. Besides, from the imposing way she held her fencing foil, I found it hard to argue.

I immediately phoned Maddie for some sympathy and was stupefied to learn that she had conspired in this debacle with my mother. It seems that before school ended, Mom was called in front of Ms. Sorin, the JFK school psychologist, who encouraged her to "give Millicent a more normal and well-rounded childhood."

As I see it, my childhood is round enough. The only thing that's wrong is that it's taking far too long for me to grow up. Where exactly does volleyball lie in the realm of my intellectual pursuits? What could I possibly learn from volleyball, other than the fact that I am uncoordinated, unpopular, and unable to see any merit in the folly of it all?

Since Maddie's gone insane and sided with my mother, I approached my father to protest the unfairness of my plight. Dad gently explained that being in a family is not always akin to being in a democracy. Then he added, "If you think you have it bad, that woman's signed me up for step aerobics."

I cannot believe my parents want me to have a "more normal childhood." I do lots of normal kid things. For instance, some of my favorite reading material includes *Archie* comics. I even bet my dad that one day Betty will displace Veronica in Archie's heart. As for other normal kid things, there are plenty of them. Like, well, I wear T-shirts and I enjoy potato chips, and I . . . well, I'm sure that if I set my mind to it, I could come up with a long list.

Anyway, if my parents are implying that I am not "normal," does that mean I am subnormal? And their brilliant solution is . . . volleyball? What is normal about forcing someone to move in rotation?

I know they are anxious for me to make friends. When I was a sophomore my grandmother encouraged me to join more extracurricular activities. She's always been a believer in groups. Maddie is a member of NOW, Greenpeace, MADD, and Costco.

Already a member of the Math Team, I joined the Chess Club, then the Latin Club. Yet even though I'm the team captain, nobody on the Math Team talks to me. The Chess Club was fun, but one by one the kids refused to play me because I always won. And the Latin Club was all right, up until I was blamed for the unfortunate "Toga Caper" as it is known around school.

It's okay, though. I know it is all somehow related to my IQ. The complex inner workings of my brain probably scare people and repel any potential friends. I suppose my lack of a wide social circle is merely an occupational hazard of genius.

That said, I am so pleased that Debbie is mature enough to

see beyond my IQ and like me for myself. We are becoming so close. Just yesterday I was telling her all about the pressures of being a child genius. "The other kids think that I'm the enemy or something," I confided.

We were in the Rogers College library and Debbie's books were strewn all over our table. "I can't help it that my teachers read my papers aloud in class or point me out as having good study habits," I continued. Debbie nodded as she examined her fingernails.

"And then," I said, lowering my voice, "there was the infamous 'Toga Caper.' I suggested to the Latin Club that we ought to wear togas during our annual 'I Love Latin' button sale. It took some convincing, but eventually I won everyone over. So on March fifteenth — that's the ides of March — we all wore the togas we made out of sheets." I took a deep breath, remembering that fateful day. "Was it my fault the French Club stole our school clothes? Was it my fault we had to wear togas for the entire day?" I looked at Debbie who was staring off into space. "Debbie?"

"Oh, right. Togas? I wore a toga once to a party. It was really fun, even though my toga had a floral pattern on it."

"As I was saying," I reminded her. "I really don't think it was my fault that our clothes got stolen. But now the entire Latin Club hates me and I am considered a persona non grata."

Debbie looked at me sympathetically. "Man, that's tough," she said. "You know what you need?"

I was hoping she'd say a chocolate milk shake.

"You need to get your mind off of togas!" Debbie flashed me a bright smile.

Or a strawberry shake, something cold would be good.

"Here, I'm going to help you." She reached for her psychology book. "Why don't we talk about my psych homework? You know, to help erase those bad thoughts you have about being in the French Club."

"The Latin Club."

"Right. The Latin Club." Debbie pointed to a passage she had highlighted in yellow. "This part here confuses me."

I didn't get my chocolate shake, but I did feel better knowing that Debbie was concerned about my feelings. I took her book and looked it over. Then together we reviewed Dr. Kuglmeier's highly regarded theory about abnormal child development.

Mom appears pleased that Debbie and I are friends, and Maddie is happy about it too. My social life seems to be of the utmost interest to both of them. I think they need hobbies.

"What do you and Debbie talk about?" Maddie asked.

"Well, we talk a lot about psychology," I said. "And Debbie's boyfriend, and we talk about the weather."

"And this Debbie," Mom inquired, "how old is she?"

"I don't know, twenty or twenty-one, I guess."

Normally, I don't like it when my mom noses around. However, I was trying to get on her good side so that she'd let me off the hook with volleyball. Unfortunately, she saw right through my little charade.

"So kind of you to do the dishes, Millicent," she noted. "And I just love that you organized the medicine cabinet. But you still have to take volleyball."

So now, in a show of good sportsmanship, and because my mother ordered me to, I am preparing for my first day of volleyball. Mom suggested I try calisthenics, but I selected another course of action.

I read up on the history of the sport, which was invented in 1895 by YMCA fitness director William G. Morgan. Then I memorized the various projections, calibrated my height against the height of the net, and even went so far as to diagram several scenarios that I thought I might share with the team.

Luckily, the outfit I am required to wear is not as awful as I had anticipated. (Do I get extra points for trying very hard to exude a positive attitude?) However, this afternoon when Mom forced me to shop for new socks and athletic shoes, I did little to mask my boredom. I hate shopping. To me, malls are monolithic icons of mass consumption and capitalism. To my mother they are nirvana.

As I laid out my uniform and reviewed tomorrow's itinerary, I wondered what it would be like to be mistaken for a jock. I have always admired those who possess superior physical dexterity and power. Jackie Joyner-Kersee's speed, strength, and stamina. Michelle Kwan's triple-lutz triple-loop combinations. Shannon Miller's full Yurchenko vaults. Perhaps I will discover my previously untapped athletic talent. After all, how hard can it be to whack a 3.759-ounce ball over the net?

If I had expected a reasonable discussion of the history of volleyball and a debate on its merits, I was wrong. Imagine my surprise when the team gathered and Coach Henrietta Gowin's first words of inspiration were "Kill them at any cost."

"Excuse me?" I raised my hand. "But aren't we here to develop camaraderie and to use the game of volleyball as a microcosm for society?"

Everyone looked at me as if I were speaking in tongues. When I was younger and my brain was on display at school or some other academic function, people were constantly poking one another and pointing at me. But as I have gotten older, the stares have lessened. And whereas I used to be called brilliant, recently I thought I heard someone call me stuck up. I did not allow it to hurt my feelings though, for it is possible I was mistaken and they were talking about someone else entirely. Yes, I think that is possible.

"Kill them at any cost," Coach Gowin snarled again, ignoring me and my question. Her dark hair was tortured into curls so tightly wound you could shoot peas through them. "Now, ladies, shall we begin?"

"Excuse me?" I ventured, raising my hand once more. I was glad I had had the foresight to bring my tape measure. "I calculated that the net is several centimeters too high, making the conditions for playing less than perfect."

Rather than thanking me, Coach Gowin, as they say in sports vernacular, "got in my face." "Millicent, I calculate that you're looking for an excuse not to play," she volleyed back. "Now get out of the bleachers and onto the floor!"

So there I was, minding my own business and wondering if I should at least pretend to be interested in the game, when the ball hit me firmly on the head. I was surprised by how much it hurt.

"Millicent, this is volleyball, not soccer!" Coach Gowin hollered. Several girls tried to suppress their snickers as I gamely attempted to expel a laugh.

As the hour plodded on, it became apparent that however precise my calculations were, the ball refused to cooperate. It didn't help that Coach Gowin kept blowing her darn whistle and shouting, "Try, Millicent! You're not even trying!"

But really, I was trying. I reviewed the movements again and again, yet no matter how much I mapped out my strategy, the ball or my body had other ideas.

When, at long last, the practice session ended, I was relieved because I had not expected to make it through the hour. I was convinced that I would need to be carried out of the gym on a stretcher, the only upside being that my mother would feel great remorse for demanding I engage in a wasted afternoon of forced fun.

"We only have one more practice session. Then we have our first game on Wednesday, and I won't be as easy on all of you," Coach Gowin threatened. "And Millicent," she sighed, "work on the basics. Don't be afraid to hit the ball. It won't bite!"

I am going to build a case against volleyball, explain to Mom that she has made a mistake, and get off the team. I can see no redeeming reason to stay on. I am clearly of no value to the team, and the game has nothing in it for me.

Volleyball reminds me of kindergarten — something I tried but was just not suited for. My mother accompanied me on my first day of school and sat in the back of the room trying to look inconspicuous. It must have been very uncomfortable for her because she was confined to one of those Lilliputian chairs and couldn't figure out what to do with her legs. (She has long legs and the body of a dancer — unlike me. I'm short and resemble a twig.)

I was assigned to a table with a girl sporting pigtails and two boys, one of whom would pee in his pants before the day was over. Most of the children in the room were crying, and one pointed to me and shrieked, "How come that baby gets to bring her mommy?"

Insulted, I informed the boy that I was not a baby, that I was three years old and would turn four in February. Unimpressed, the boy stuck his tongue out at me. When I began to chide his infantile behavior, I stopped myself. Really, it is impossible to argue with a child.

Turning her back to the commotion, the teacher wrote her name on the chalkboard in big fat letters. When she finished, she smiled and spoke through her teeth. "My name is Miss Carp," she said loudly, as if we were geriatrics, not juveniles.

Being helpful, I shared with the class that carp can flourish in muddy water. Before I could even begin to describe their skeletal system, the pigtailed girl yelled, "Teacher rolls around in the mud!"

As the whole class burst out laughing, Miss Carp looked alarmed, like she had just swallowed a fly.

I tried to make it up to her the rest of the day by answering anytime she asked the class a question. Or by team-teaching with her when she seemed at a loss, which was quite often. I do think that despite the weary look on her face, which grew worse whenever I raised my hand, Miss Carp thought highly of me. After all, the minute the 3:30 bell rang, she pulled my mother aside, told her I was very bright for my age, and suggested I skip a grade.

I wonder if Debbie's ever skipped a grade? I put it on my list of topics to discuss with her the next time I see her. And volleyball, boy, I can't wait to tell her about volleyball.

Despite my detailed analysis of what was wrong with Craig (see list), Debbie started seeing him again.

Craig's Shortcomings

1. Immature	6. Wears same T-shirt several days in a row
2. Selfish	7. Hogs conversation
3. Has changed major 5 times	8. Thinks Jane Austen is a country singer
4. Always late	9. Poor table manners
5. Never has exact change	10. Chews his pen

At first we'd all study together, but I know I made him nervous, especially after he found the list. Unfortunately, by then Debbie was under his spell.

"Millie, do you mind?" Debbie said this afternoon, folding up what I can only discern was a love letter. It was written on the back of a flyer advertising kickboxing lessons. "It's personal, okay?" I stopped reading over her shoulder, but not before seeing the vomit-inducing clichés "Can't live without you" and "You are the sunshine of my life."

Debbie looked over my head and surveyed the cafeteria. "Don't you have any other friends?" she asked.

"Nope," I said. I was happy that she considered me a friend. "Not here, anyway. My best friend is Maddie," I told her, leaving out the part about Maddie being my grandmother.

"Hey, Deb," I asked. I was a little bit apprehensive. "How would you like to go to the movies with me sometime? Or maybe you could come to my house for dinner. My mom says it would be okay."

"Oh, Millie," Debbie said, sighing deeply. We were having mocha lattes and sipping off the foam. (Well, actually I was having a root beer, she was having a mocha latte.) "Listen, I'm very fond of you, but you're just a child. You can't really expect us to be in the same social circle, can you?"

I felt like I was having a sudden asthma attack, only I don't have asthma. Immediately, Debbie began waving her arms and yelling, "Over here!" I was touched that she was calling for medical assistance. Until I realized that she was signaling Craig to come join us.

"I thought we were friends and that you liked talking about college, and the mean kids in high school, and the stupidity of volleyball," I blurted out as I tried to catch my breath.

Craig dragged a chair over and sat between us. "I like volley-ball," he offered as he slurped Debbie's latte through three coffee stirrers.

"Hey!" she said in mock anger.

Craig grinned and began to kiss her. Disgusting. I just scowled at him. Mid-kiss, they both opened their eyes and stared back at me. "Are you still here?" Craig asked.

Debbie pushed him away. "Not now," she whispered.

He wrapped his arms around her. "Debbie's not your baby-sitter, you know," he said. "She only lets you hang around be-cause you do her homework and she feels sorry for you."

I was aghast. Okay, so maybe we weren't in the same social circle. But at least we were friends, anyone could see that. "Deb-bie," I said, glaring at Craig. "Tell him that's not true!" Debbie looked at me, and then at Craig, and then back at me. "Tell him," I insisted.

"Millie . . . I'm sorry," she began.

I didn't wait to hear what else she had to say. Without a word, I got up, gathered my things, and tried to make a dramatic exit, only I bumped into Craig's chair and hurt my hip. As I hob-bled away, Debbie began to call after me, but Craig hushed her. Then I heard him telling her that I was a freak. To her credit, Debbie defended me and told him that he was just jealous.

Imagine that. Jealous of a freak.

Okay, so maybe I have been brooding over the way Debbie treated me. And maybe I did retreat to my tree and refuse to come down for dinner last night. Still, you'd think that my parents would have sympathy for me. But nooooo. Instead they are adding to my anguish.

"You want me to what?" I bellowed for a second time. I feared I was starting to lose my hearing and would end up deaf like Ludwig van Beethoven.

"I want you to tutor Stanford Wong," my mother said again. She looked tired. Perhaps coaxing me down from my tree had sapped her strength. Not enough, unfortunately, to stop her from lobbing another zinger my way.

I turned to my father, who was absorbed in rooting around for his prize in the Cracker Jack box. When he was a kid he won a Winky Badge and has been searching for another plastic rabbit like it ever since.

With this glaring absence of insight from my father on the

Stanford situation, I was forced to ponder my fate alone. Stanford Wong is the poster boy for Chinese geekdom and the grandson of one of Maddie's many best friends. I hadn't seen my nemesis in months, and that was not long enough for me.

The last time I was in the same room with Stanford he was squatting behind a chair stuffing his face with pineapple during a game of "Catch the Castaway" at my ill-fated eleventh birthday party. Wearing his regular uniform of jeans, white T-shirt, Lakers cap, and thick glasses, he poisoned my house with his mere presence. Later, when I saw him marching my way gritting his teeth, I knew that he was being sent over to talk to me. I started to back away, but hit the kitchen wall. There was nowhere to turn. Nowhere to run.

"Milli-scent," he said without much enthusiasm.

"Stan-turd," I replied.

We both looked over to our grandmothers, who were waving and giving each other so many little nudges that one of them was bound to tip over at any moment. Stanford and I smiled back and then resumed glaring at each other. We have had this routine since we were small.

"You're ruining it for the rest of us," he hissed. "Stop it."

"Ruining what?"

"Our lives."

"Stink-ford, I have no idea what you are talking about."

He pitched his voice so that it sounded singsongy. "Whizzing though elementary school, practically skipping middle school, starting high school at the tender young age of nine. Because of you, teachers expect every Chinese kid to be a genius."

I looked at him standing there with a permanent grimace plastered on his face. Perhaps what he said is true. Stanford is not a genius. Far from it. According to Maddie, he gets bad grades, is a goof-off in class, and has little aptitude for academics, although, she is always quick to add, his penmanship is excellent.

"I will try my best to do worse," I muttered before walking away. "I'll simply use you as my role model."

And now this. I am to tutor my mortal enemy. When we spoke on the phone, Stanford was none too thrilled about the prospect either. In fact, his first words were, and I quote, "Aw, this sucks."

According to Maddie, there is no way he is going to make it through the sixth grade on his own. He failed his English class and has to retake it in summer school. Stanford is expected to write three book reports, plus pass all his quizzes and a final exam, if he is to move up to the seventh grade. That's where I come in. Maddie had been boasting about me to Stanford's grandmother, who told Stanford's father, who told Stanford's mother, who asked my mother if I would consider tutoring her son. Then, without even consulting me, my mother agreed that starting next Thursday I would commence tutoring Knucklehead.

"Maddie and I thought this would help get your mind off Debbie," Mom tried to reason with me.

Right. "Hey!" I said. "How about just hitting me over the head with a shovel? That would take my mind off Debbie and be a lot less painful."

Dad started to chuckle, but my mother silenced him with a glare.

My summer schedule is filling up fast. So far, here it is . . .

MON:	College Poetry	9:30–11:30 A.M.
	Volleyball	1:00–3:00 P.M.
	Stupid Stanford	3:30–4:30 P.M.
TUE:	Stupid Stanford	3:30–4:30 P.M.
WED:	College Poetry	9:30–11:30 A.M.
	Volleyball	1:00–3:00 P.M.
THU:	Stupid Stanford	3:30–4:30 P.M.
FRI:	College Poetry	9:30–11:30 A.M.
	Volleyball	1:00–3:00 P.M.
SAT:	Volleyball	10:00 A.M–Noon
SUN:	Recover and begin again	

I wonder what my parents have planned for me next? Maybe they'll loan me out to clean septic tanks. Or perhaps I'll be sold to the National Hockey League and used as a puck.

If there is any upside to this bad Stanford joke, it is that I will get paid for tutoring. Ever since my dad got laid off, money has been really tight. I am not supposed to say he was fired. Just that he's now a "contract engineer." Sometimes his jobs last five months, sometimes a week. He loves this and says he does not like to be constrained, but it makes Mom really antsy and her coupon clipping has increased tenfold.

My parents quarrel about money. They think I don't know, but I have a Littmann Electronic Model 2000 stethoscope with an extended frequency range of 100–1,000 Hz. It works really well against the wall.

When they have a fight they become excruciatingly polite to each other and adopt a false cheerfulness, the kind usually reserved for laundry detergent commercials in the scene where they get the spot out. What's worse, they behave as if it's "Be Kind to Millicent Day," showering me with false compliments and sneaking me cookies before dinner. As if my vote counted.

Maybe I ought to just live in my tree. When I am up here, I can just be myself, by myself. Here, I don't have to contend with Maddie asking, "Millie, are you still sad about Debbie?" Or Dad quipping, "Who needs her when you have your good ol' Dad?" Or Mom saying, "Cheer up, Millie. I'm sure you'll make new friends. You just have to try a little harder."

If they are really so concerned about me, then they would get me out of volleyball and out of tutoring Stanford Wong.

Despite my compelling arguments, my mother does not agree with the fresh new direction I suggested my summer activities take. In fact, she even threatened that if I did not stop complaining ("whining" was the term she used), she would also enroll me in synchronized swimming. Thus, it was with great reluctance that I showed up for volleyball again. Luckily, I was already on a team and did not have to suffer the indignity of being chosen last. There's enough of that at school.

The game began auspiciously enough with the ball flying back and forth, unless, of course, it came anywhere in my vicinity. When it was my turn to serve, I somehow managed to make the ball go behind me. This produced a great deal of tittering from both sides of the net. Embarrassed, I moved forward and prayed that the gym would catch fire or that the ball would explode.

A rather tall, scary girl from the other team took her place to serve. She looked like she could squish me like a bug. Grinning, the girl tossed the ball up in the air with ease. Then she smashed it in the desired direction.

I squeezed my eyes shut as the ball came barreling down at me in what seemed like slow motion. As I said a prayer, I wondered if this was how the dinosaurs felt when the giant asteroid came screaming toward Earth.

Suddenly, *BANG*! Contact. To everyone's amazement, I sent the ball flying back to enemy territory. It landed at the feet of the server and then bounced away.

There was a stunned silence as jaws dropped in unison.

Then, at once, laughter erupted. It echoed in the gym and I am sure could be heard throughout Rancho Rosetta.

"She kicked the ball!" someone howled.

I could have just died.

Somehow I managed to struggle through the rest of the

game. Not making eye contact with anyone helped, although I am sure my teammates were miffed that I kept bumping into them.

When at last the game was over, I plopped down against the bleachers. I rummaged through my briefcase and fished out a bag of Cheetos and a Gatorade. After I tried in vain to twist the cap off my drink, the girl sitting next to me took the bottle from me and opened it on the first try. Of course, I'm sure I had loosened it quite a bit.

I studied the bottle opener and recognized her as one of the few who did not laugh at me. If I had thought practice was bad, it was nothing compared to my first game. I am convinced my kick will become legendary. Plus, I had barely survived the arrogance, competitiveness, and name-calling. And that was from my own team.

"Hi," the girl said.

I was cautious, for I thought she might want to chide me for my lackluster performance.

"How do you do?" I answered with some trepidation.

"I'm Emily and I just moved here. Don't you hate volleyball? Isn't Coach Gowin just awful? She reminds me of a potato with toothpick legs. Wouldn't you just love to get your hands on whoever gave her that whistle?"

She paused for a breath, and I seized the chance to get a word in. "I'm Millicent L. Min. Yes. Yes. Ha! Yes," I replied, as I wiped my palm in anticipation of a more formal introduction and a handshake.

You can tell a lot about a person by the way they shake hands. Some people try to crush your bones to prove that they're in control. Others barely move their hands and make you do all the work. Then there's the firm, friendly "hello-there-sincerely-glad-to-meet-you" handshake that I strive to achieve. My mother and I practiced for weeks until I got it right.

The girl tossed formalities aside and continued chatting. I smiled and waited patiently to find out why she thought we were friends. To my delight, I was surprisingly at ease with Emily. There was no pretense, just good-natured social interaction. On two separate occasions we found ourselves finishing each other's sentences. It was so liberating to talk with someone my own age without the topic of my being a genius coming up and getting in the way.

As we were deep in conversation, a throng of girls sauntered past us. "Keep her away from the doughnuts," one of them joked as she looked directly at Emily. Everyone laughed, including Emily, but I could tell she really didn't think it was all that funny. Emily isn't what I'd call fat, but she definitely wasn't like the tall lanky gorgeous girls on our team. Neither was I.

"That's a good one," Emily called out. "Thanks for the advice, but actually, I only eat healthy food!" I looked at my

Cheetos and quickly sat on the bag before Emily could see them.

I didn't know what to say to Emily about the fat attack she had just endured. It's one thing to come up with clever comebacks when you are being verbally assaulted, but quite another to devise witty retorts on behalf of someone you just met. To my relief Emily filled up the awkward silence.

"My mom thinks volleyball will be good for me. You know, get coordinated and meet new people, blah, blah, blah," she confided as she let down her ponytail and shook it out.

Emily reached into her backpack and pulled out a Snickers bar. She offered me half. "I thought you only ate healthy food," I said, biting into it.

"I just said that to make her feel bad," Emily remarked with a sly grin. "I know I could stand to lose a few pounds, but the doctor said that I'm healthy, so what's the big deal? So tell me, why are you here? No offense, but you didn't look like you enjoyed yourself at all. In fact, a couple of times I thought you were going to cry."

I could have explained that because I went through school at an accelerated rate, I was never expected to fully participate in physical education. Yet if Emily knew I was a genius she might weird out on me like the rest of them. In a nanosecond I had to decide whether to tell the truth and risk losing a potential friend, or lie and live with the consequences.

Four years ago I spoke at a conference on gifted children. My mother and I got to fly to Chicago, the Windy City. We stayed at a big, impressive hotel with full-grown trees in the lobby. There was only one other kid my age at the conference, so everyone kept pushing us at each other. The boy was really cocky, and he loved using big words to confound and impress the adults. I couldn't stand him.

Finally, I said, "You are so full of yourself, I'll bet you don't even have any friends." To which he retorted, "I'll bet you don't have any friends!" Then we both stood there with our hands on our hips trying to come up with a witty reply. Because the truth was, neither of us had any friends.

It's not that I don't try. Didn't I make a valiant effort to befriend Debbie? Nonetheless, that friendship was probably doomed from the start due to 1) the interference of Craig, her moronic boyfriend; and 2) Debbie's incapacity to see past my ability to do her psychology homework in record time.

At the gifted children conference, I attempted a cartwheel in the hallway when no one was looking. I like to bring that up when people accuse me of not being fun and spontaneous.

I looked over at Emily, who was grinning at me as if in anticipation of a witty remark. "I don't have gym, I'm home-schooled," I heard myself saying. "So my parents want me to get more exercise, even though I'm not really into sports."

"Me too!" Emily squealed. "I just hate organized sports, it's so competitive."

Just then, Julie, the team captain, broke away from the pack and sauntered over. Or should I say "sashayed"? Well, whatever it was, it didn't seem like normal walking, more like what the mean-faced models do on the catwalk. With her looks and the way she carried herself, Julie could have been a model. I knew that and so did she.

Amazingly, as I shrank in her presence, Emily seemed to get taller. Julie checked us out and without hiding her disdain said, "I hope you two won't hold the team back this year. Most of us played together last year, and we almost won first place."

I am used to this sort of talk. Just by looking at me you can see that I am not Olympic material. You know how they say, "Sticks and stones can break your bones, but words will never hurt you"? Well, it's not true. Still, Emily brushed off Julie's comment in a way I could not help but admire. I'm not sure if she even knew she was being slammed.

"We're going to try our best," Emily said, smiling. "Right, Millie?" She nudged me in the ribs.

"Uh, right," I concurred.

Julie stood with her hands on her bony hips, as if she could not decide what to make of Emily. "Good," she finally said, faltering a bit. "We all really want to win, that's all."

"We want to win too," Emily said, wearing Julie down by the sheer force of her upbeat personality. "We'll try hard, if you promise to try hard too."

"Uh . . . yeah, sure," Julie said, looking confused. "I promise."

"Jules, come on," one of the other girls huffed. "This is sooooo boring."

As Julie was once again enveloped by her clique, Emily and I were left alone. For a while we sat in silence. I wasn't sure what I had just witnessed, but it was impressive. Then Emily spoke up.

"Hey, do you mind if I ask you a personal question?"

Okay, here it comes, I thought. She must have heard I was a genius. Well, so long potential friend, it was nice knowing you. "What?" I said, waiting for the inevitable.

"Why are you sitting on your Cheetos?"

Embarrassed, I started laughing and so did she. "I don't know, sometimes I just do weird things," I said, pulling the bag out from under me.

"Me too." Emily grinned. "Hey, wanna go get some ice cream? Or we could hang out at my house, my dad just bought me a new Be-Dazzler."

How could I tell her that I had to prepare my first lesson plan for stupid Stanford Wong? That I was a genius trapped in the body of an eleven-year-old? That I had no clue what a Be-Dazzler was?

"Um, sorry. Not today," I said. Emily looked dejected, like a puppy being sent away. "But how about some other time?" I asked.

"Really?" she said instantly. "I'd love to!"

"Me too," I said, returning her smile.

The prospect of having a friend my own age is quite thrilling. I hope Emily will not be put off by my credentials. After all, with Debbie my IQ clouded our friendship. I will tell Emily the truth the next time I see her. In the meantime, I have to deal with the Stanford Predicament.

It isn't just that Stanford is stupid, it's that he's spectacularly stupid. Words float in through one ear and out the other. Books go unread. And spelling is a total farce. Or as he would write, "farse."

We agreed to meet on common ground, the Bruggemeyer Public Library periodical section. I doubt if Stanford even knows what a periodical is. He probably thinks it's what happens to girls when they reach a certain age.

As expected, I was there first with twelve minutes to spare.

"Millicent," Mrs. Martinez looked up from the return desk. "I haven't seen you for a while. I was getting worried."

With great pride I explained that I was now a student at

Rogers College (I neglected to tell her it was only one class) and was frequenting the campus library. "I'm just meeting someone here," I said, sounding vague, yet hoping I gave enough information so that she would not ask me any more questions. Luckily, a woman showed up with several overdue Tom Clancy books and I was able to escape.

I selected an out-of-the-way table between the periodicals and 900 Geo-Hist and settled in, lining up my pens, notebook, clock, and lesson plan in front of me.

Twenty-four minutes later, *clomp, clomp, clomp.* I could hear Stanford before I could see him. Even though I hid behind a Harry Houdini biography, Stanford spotted me.

"Nerd."

"Geek."

"Imbecile."

"Freak."

After a few minutes of this, I realized that I was the tutor, the one in the position of authority, and I could not allow it to continue. Plus, I was being paid seven dollars an hour — the same rate as a baby-sitter — to make Stanford smarter. If Maddie ever finds out that I called him names, she won't take me to R-rated movies anymore.

"Stanford," I said. "Let's get past this and move on to the real reason you are here, shall we?"

He slumped down in his chair as if his spine had suddenly

collapsed. I don't know what is more painful, tutoring Stanford or being whacked on the head with a volleyball.

"Listen," he said, finally sitting up and making furtive glances around the room. "You gotta promise me you won't tell anyone about this."

"About this what?" I asked, annoyed. I noticed he hadn't even brought a pen. The only thing he had with him was a basketball, like that was really going to help him here.

"This tutoring business."

"Yeah, okay," I said, opening my briefcase and pulling out my backup pens. I wasn't about to let him use one of my good ones. "Now tell me, what is it about reading that you find so difficult?"

"NO!" he shouted, startling both of us. Mrs. Martinez almost dropped an armload of books. "No," he said more softly through gritted teeth. "You have to swear you won't tell."

His request was ridiculous and so was he. As if I'd want anyone to know I tutor a monkey brain, or that I'd even have someone to tell. Suddenly, I thought of Emily. If Emily ever connects me to Stanford she might discover that I am a genius, albeit a tortured one. Tutoring Stanford is as close to torture as I have ever come.

"All right. I won't tell," I finally said.

"Cross your heart and hope to die, stick a needle in your eye," he said solemnly.

"This is ridiculous. Why don't we just spit into our palms and rub them together?" I scoffed.

"Oh, I hadn't thought of that!" Stanford spit into his hands and held them out to me.

Horrified, I declared, "I'd rather eat worms!"

Stanford's eyes lit up, and he said in a rush, "I've eaten a worm before. I ate it on a dare, and it didn't taste half bad. It wasn't as chewy as I thought it would be. . . ." Before he could finish his tale of culinary curiosity, I got up and did a slow lap around the periodicals. Tutoring was going to be a lot harder than I had anticipated. How could I possibly expect Stanford to write three book reports and pass a final exam?

At last, we agreed to sign a document attesting to our secret. To show our sincerity, I swore on my mother's life that I would not tell a soul, and Stanford promised to bring some paper and a decent pen to our next session. That done, we were finally free to begin.

"Maddie says you goof off in class," I told him, flipping to a blank page in my college-ruled spiral-bound notebook. I love blank pages, they hold so much promise. "She said your grandmother told her so."

"Great." He slumped down. "My grandmother tells everyone my business. She expects me to be a scholar, and then to make things worse, I'm always being compared to you. *You*, of all people. Can you imagine the humiliation of that?" He raised his voice in what I could only hope was a bad imitation of his grandmother. " 'Why can't you be more like Millicent Min, that nice, smart Chinese girl,' she's always saying. Well, excuse me for living!"

"I'm trying to," I muttered.

As much as I hated Stanford, I could commiserate with being the victim of an unwarranted comparison. A lot of people expect that since I am Chinese I should behave in a certain way. Just today, when I ordered the huevos rancheros (yum) at the Rogers College cafeteria, the cashier looked at me and said, "I didn't think you people liked that kind of food."

Nothing like being lumped in with a billion other people.

So I said to her, "Well, we can't eat rice all the time." She thought a moment and said, "Yeah, I guess you're right."

"What are you doing now?" I hissed to Stanford.

"Eating a deviled-ham sandwich," he said, oblivious to his surroundings and the glob of mystery meat on his chin. "I have to keep my energy up for basketball. I'm the league free-throw champion," he said, like it was something I should already know.

"Put that away right now!" I ordered. "Or we'll get kicked out of here."

"Chill, Mill." Stanford took another bite in slow motion to torture me. "You want a taste?" He dangled the offending object in front of my face.

I would never consider eating deviled ham, much less anything Stanford offered me that hadn't been tested in a laboratory.

As Stanford munched and I stewed, I could not believe how out of control my summer had become. I had everything so well planned and now here I was, rejected by Debbie, the laughing-stock of the volleyball league, and tutor to the unteachable.

I stared at Stanford who, having consumed a bag of mesquite barbecue chips, was now draining a can of Mountain Dew. He grinned at me and then let out a huge belch. It was more than I could bear. I stood up and threw my organizer at him, but missed. "You pig," I shouted. "You have no regard for anyone but yourself!"

Stanford looked surprised. Mrs. Martinez sprinted over to me and laid her hand on my shoulder just as I was about to bean him over the head with my *Webster's*.

"Millicent," she said, pausing to gasp for air, "please lower your voice. This is a library, not a playground." She pried the dictionary from my hands and placed it on the table. "I expect better of you."

Stanford began to snicker until Mrs. Martinez began lecturing him on the evils of eating food in the library. Slowly, he started slouching in his chair, making his way toward the floor until all I could see of him was the top of his hollow head.

The good news first or the bad news?

I like to start with bad news because it leaves something to look forward to. I think Maddie's under the negative influence of my parents. When I approached her about the absurdity of my continuing to tutor Stanford Wong, she refused even to consider my point of view. Maddie went so far as to report she heard that I had disrupted the quiet of the library and that Stanford felt I hadn't taught him a thing. I can't believe Maddie has turned into Benedict Arnold.

Dejected, I sat in my tree with my *Norton Anthology of Poetry.* As I glanced across the street, I noticed something odd. Five-year-old Max was sneaking out onto the ledge of an upstairs window. I wondered what mischief he was up to this time and whether he has ever considered the consequences of his actions.

With a great flourish, Max unfurled an oversize red umbrella and held it high above his head. Just as he was about to jump, his mother appeared at the window. She ordered him back inside and then slammed the window shut, letting the umbrella fall unaccompanied to the ground.

I had just opened my book to Emily Brontë's *The Prisoner* when my mother came outside, holding the phone aloft as if it were an Oscar. "Millie, it's for you," she shouted, looking pleased with herself. (I never get any phone calls.)

Now the good news . . .

"Hi, Millie. It's me!" someone squealed. I held the receiver away from my ear and examined it to make sure I wasn't hearing feedback.

"Me who?" I asked politely. My mother and I have a policy never to accept phone solicitations. Dad bought our hot tub that way. It remains docked in the garage and doubles as storage vessel for the festive holiday decorations of which my mother is so fond.

"It's me, Emily. Wanna come over to my house for a sleepover on Tuesday?"

A mixture of elation and panic swept over me.

"Hello? Hello, Millie are you there?"

A sleepover? I liked Emily well enough, and had even mused about what our friendship might entail. But what if she were some sort of juvenile delinquent or something? After all, Debbie had turned into an entirely different person once her true colors were revealed. Plus, how could I ever forget my pseudo-friendships at Star Brite?

I attended Star Brite, the elite private school, soon after I was expelled from Rancho Rosetta Elementary. It was Boynton Wilson who fessed up. He was on the verge of being kicked out for throwing firecrackers into the girls' bathroom. Boynton was always on the verge of something.

Life at Star Brite was rosier than at public school. The bathrooms were cleaner, the teachers were calmer, and the lockers opened on the first try. And at lunchtime, there seemed to be no limit to the number of students who sought me out in the cafeteria. Sometimes they even fought over me saying, "Hey, today I'm supposed to sit next to Millicent."

This clamoring for my company made me feel good, even if we hardly spoke during lunch. I had observed other kids palling around with their friends and talking nonstop, but I assumed that my lunchtime friendships were on a much deeper level. So deep that words were not necessary.

Over sandwiches one day, Boynton blurted out, "Why don't you ever say anything? She said you were a good role model and that if maybe we spent some time with you, it'll rub off."

He helped himself to my strawberries, even though I had not offered him any.

"What are you blathering about?" I asked as I examined my peanut butter. Mom had bought the chunky kind because it was on sale. I prefer creamy.

"Mrs. Murphy, the guidance counselor," Boynton said with

his mouth full. "She said we'd do well to hang out with you. That we might actually learn something and that our efforts would be noted on our permanent records."

"You were told to eat with me?" I asked.

Boynton nodded and eyed the rest of my lunch. Although he was from one of the wealthiest families in Rancho Rosetta, Boynton had the manners and the scent of a goat. It was common knowledge that it was not his dedication to learning that kept Boynton at Star Brite, but his family's money. It helped fund the new gymnasium and afforded scholarships to students like me.

As I let the weight of Boynton's information sink in, I handed over my sandwich. The chunky peanut butter was upsetting my stomach anyway.

"Are you there? Millie, are you still there?" someone yelled. "Hellooooo . . . ?"

I was surprised to find the phone in my hand. "I'm still here," I said.

"I'm afraid we might have a bad connection," I heard Emily say.

"No, no. The connection's just fine," I assured her.

"Okay, then, as I was saying, if you don't want to come to my house, maybe I can come to yours," Emily offered.

She has no idea how peculiar my parents are. "I don't think that's a good idea," I started to say before she cut me off.

"Then it's settled, you'll come here. Oh, wait!" Emily shouted.

"My mom wants to talk to your mom. . . ." Great. Now she was getting the moms involved. Once moms are involved there is no turning back.

I must admit, I am intrigued by the thought of my first sleepover. And Emily seems like a decent person, albeit a little too enthusiastic. Still, she's friendly, and the truth is I am curious as to what it would be like to have a friend in my age range.

Yet what exactly does a sleepover involve? Of course, technically, I sleep over at Maddie's all the time. Yet with Emily, I would be interjecting myself into a new environment and perhaps even setting myself up for disaster. For example, what if I was expected to sleep on the floor? I have observed that girls sleep on the floor at sleepovers, at least that's what Jan, Marcia, and Cindy from *The Brady Bunch* do. Not that I ever watch the show, but it is a favorite of my parents' since they are from that era.

I really don't want to sleep on the floor. I don't think it would be good for my back. And what about towels? Should I bring my own? Do I bring my own shampoo and tartar-control toothpaste? There was so much to think about.

Our moms talked for half an hour (ostensibly to say "hello," but really to check each other out) and ended up making plans for lunch.

Mom makes friends easily. On the phone. In the Ten Items or Less line. A few years ago when we were at the Grand Canyon, she befriended an entire busload of German tourists when they got separated from their tour guide. Every Christmas we still get boxes of homemade bratwurst.

"Well, Millicent, you made quite a deep impression on Emily. You will be a gracious guest, won't you?" my mother asked as she hung up.

I was so relieved. I was afraid that if Emily stayed at my house our burgeoning friendship would be cut short the first time my father balanced a peanut on his nose.

My mom's birthday is coming up, so as a gift, I'm going to let her take me shopping and not complain the entire time. She will be delighted. I need pajamas. Right now I sleep in an old shirt of Grandpa's that reads "War is not healthy for children and other living things." I love it because it reminds me of him, but it's full of holes and I wouldn't want Emily to think we are poor.

Though I am excited about the sleepover, I plan to be cautious about our developing friendship. If I'm not careful, something could go wrong again.

Mom was thrilled that I let her take me shopping. She bought me a nightgown with clouds all over it and a pajama set covered with polka dots. Both were forty percent off. We disagreed over whether the clouds were stratocumulus, which are basically layered cumulus, as I said, or cirrus. However, we were in total agreement that the polka dots were just colorful circles.

When we got home, Maddie and my father were waiting with a glorious chocolate cake covered in yellow buttercream frosting and topped with red rosettes and plastic dinosaurs. "I made it myself," Maddie said, feigning a blush.

She then presented Mom with an attractive beaded purse. Tucked inside was a gift certificate to my mother's favorite shoe store. Dad and I gave her a wooden model of a stegosaurus and a book called *Fossil Feud: The Rivalry of the First American Dinosaur Hunters.* Although Mom is an actuary, her long-term goal is to obtain a master's degree in paleontology. Mom loves dinosaurs. Which is why, she says, she married Dad.

Mom was so happy and that made me happy. When I am in my tree, if I lean forward and to the left, I can look directly into the living room. I've spied my mom moping around the house a lot lately. With my binoculars I can see into most of the neighbors' houses too. You'd be surprised at what people do when they think no one is watching.

After cake and ice cream (two helpings of each), I retreated to my room and opened *1,001 Jokes.* I will have to tell Mrs. Martinez that the title is misleading. There aren't really 1,001 jokes in the book, but only 473.

I placed Post-it notes on the jokes I thought were appropriate for girls my age and then set about memorizing them. Then I drew up a list of potential topics to explore with Emily. They included: 1) History of the Be-Dazzler (I found out it is a clever sewing apparatus designed to fasten rhinestones and studs to clothing); 2) volleyball: elevating or enervating?; and 3) Joan of Arc and other misunderstood adolescents like ourselves.

As I sat in my room practicing a spontaneous laugh, my mother came in carrying yet another load of laundry. She's fanatic about clean laundry and washes bath towels after one use. "What's so funny, Millie?"

I clamped my mouth shut and slid the joke book beneath my poetry homework. "Nothing," I said. "I was just rereading *A Midsummer Night's Dream.*"

Mom loaded up the washing machine and then eased herself onto the floor with me. "I had a great day, sweetheart," she said. I liked the smell of her. It was like soap and summer.

"Me too, Mom."

She leaned her head against my shoulder. "Are you happy, Millicent?"

I gave it some consideration. I was really looking forward to my upcoming sleepover, and Professor Skylanski had hinted about a pop quiz. Pop quizzes are so much fun. "Let me think," I said, pausing. "Yes, I believe I am. Are you?"

Mom got a faraway look in her eyes. "Happier than I ever imagined," she murmured. Then she kissed me on the forehead and left me with my jokes and the soothing sound of the washing machine chugging away.

In spite of the constant grumbling from the other students, poetry class is a pleasure. Professor Skylanski is brilliant, and I feel a natural kinship with her. At the close of today's class, I joked that we were a "couplet" of huge poetry fans. She replied, "*Iamb* sure of that!" causing us both to fall into a fit of hysterics that was further exacerbated when I inadvertently let out a snort.

Unfortunately, my happiness was short-lived when I overheard one of my fellow students mutter, "Nothing like being the teacher's pet. Just who does little Miss Smarty-Pants think she is?" To which another student replied, "Well, she's certainly not one of us."

Where do I belong, then? I began to panic thinking about Emily's sleepover. This is my big chance to make a friend, a true friend. What if Emily rejects me like Debbie did? Then it will be back to just Maddie and me. At least I'll always have Maddie.

My grandparents met when they were kids. You'd think they

would have grown tired of each other. But even when they quarreled, which was often, they still could not bear to be apart.

After Grandpa died, I would go to Maddie's house and find her sitting by the window. "We were like this," Maddie once said as she linked her fingers together. "Now I am only half of what I used to be." Her hands fell into her lap as she stared outside. I could not see what she was looking at.

Maddie selected an old Chinese poem called "The Worn Path" to be read at Grandpa's funeral. From time to time, when she gets wistful, she asks me to recite it. "I miss my partner in crime," she says.

Just recently, Maddie's shroud of sadness lifted. "Whew," she said this afternoon, patting her forehead with Grandpa's handkerchief as if she had been in the sun too long. "That's enough self-pity to smother a horse." I looked up from my *1,001 Jokes.* "Grandpa could never stand a self-pitier, and I don't suppose he's been looking at me fondly. It's time to celebrate his life, not mourn his death," she said, trying to smile.

Still, I can tell when she is sad. Maddie gets sad a lot when she thinks about him.

"You know," Maddie said, trying to cheer *me* up, "from all you've told me, your grandfather would have adored Emily." I was trying out my jokes on her, but getting frustrated since half of the time she couldn't tell when I had gotten to the punch line. "He was convinced you'd have lots and lots of friends. 'That little Millie,' he'd say to me. 'So much going for her. Someday she'll be the most popular girl at the ball.'"

My grandfather. What a dreamer.

When I first told Maddie about meeting Emily, she proclaimed the stars had aligned to form a new constellation. Maybe she was right about that one. Except for the fact that my new friend is loquacious, blonde, and Jewish, Emily and I are exactly the same.

Maddie let me borrow one of her suitcases for the sleepover. She has a full set from the Home Shopping Network. Since Grandpa died, she's been having trouble sleeping. So instead she buys a lot of things from those chronically effervescent people hawking their goods on television. Maddie's been on the air twice, once expounding about the merits of the ThrillGrill Mini-Frying Pan, and another time to give a heartfelt testimonial about cubic zirconia. She did really well considering she doesn't own either of them.

I packed both sets of new pajamas, two extra sets of clothes, my first-aid kit, assorted toiletries, and my allergy medication. Then I stood before the mirror and gathered my nerve to let out a spontaneous laugh. It sounded pretty good, so I tried one more.

I think I'm ready.

Emily was waiting in the driveway when my mother dropped me off. She grabbed my suitcase and dragged me into the house. "Oh Millie! I am so excited. You are my very first guest," she gushed.

Emily's enthusiasm was making me nervous, and I was afraid that she might start hugging me. I am not a hugger, which is ironic considering that my parents have no qualms about public displays of affection. I looked over my shoulder at my mother, sitting in the Volvo talking with Emily's mother. Mom winked at me, and I gave her a weak wave back.

As I entered the house, I was immediately struck by the books. There were books everywhere, a reader's paradise. Emily's mom came in and saw me eyeing them. "Please forgive me for all the books," she said. How could anyone be sorry about having so many books? "I know it's a mess, but I just haven't gotten around to organizing yet."

There were rows and rows of books on economics and

literature and world history lining the shelves. Even more books were stacked in short piles on the floor and many were open as if someone had just set them down momentarily. On the walls were framed magazine covers and articles.

"You're Alice X. Ebers, the journalist?" I squawked. I was a great fan of hers and was especially moved by her series in the *Atlantic Monthly* on child labor.

"Yes, I'm that Alice X. Ebers," Emily's mom said, looking at me with a mixture of surprise and curiosity. "Although around here I'm just plain Alice. You know of my work?"

I froze. To say yes would reveal my high intellect and voracious reading that far surpassed the interests of an ordinary eleven-year-old. I looked at Emily, who was staring at me with an odd expression on her face. I've seen that look before when I speak up in class or when test results are announced.

"My mom mentioned that you wrote," I mumbled. Emily looked relieved, and Alice looked disappointed.

"Well, that makes sense," Alice remarked. "My readership is skewed more toward graduate students and pseudo-intellectuals than middle-school girls, right, Emily?" Emily ignored her. "The only thing I write that Emily ever reads are the notes I leave on the kitchen counter. And I suspect that even those go unread," Alice said, laughing.

Emily took my arm. "Come on," she said, leading me away. "Let's get out of here!" I wanted to stay and talk to her mom about writing, and I think Alice would have liked that too. Yet in Emily's eyes I was a normal girl. And normal girls don't talk about those sort of things. Normal girls talk about . . . well, just what *do* they talk about? I'm going to have to research that.

Emily lives in an enormous tract house with central heat and air, cable TV, and two gas fireplaces. "This place is huge," I whispered reverently as Emily gave me the house tour. I couldn't help but notice they even had books in the bathroom and laundry room.

"Yeah," she said, not sounding the least bit impressed. "Alice claims we moved to California to get as far away from my dad as possible." Emily lowered her voice. "But she still thinks he's going to come to his senses and return someday. So she bought this place because he always said he wanted a big house on the West Coast. Go figure."

Emily's mom is absolutely wonderful. So avant garde. She insisted I call her by her first name. Alice's smile is warm and her eyes sparkle. Although Emily vehemently denies it, she looks just like her. Alice wore denim with some sort of medieval-looking blouse and served frozen dinners and iced tea from a can.

"It's fascinating that you're a journalist," I told Alice when I was in the middle of my Three-Cheese Stuffed Rigatoni. Emily was just poking at her Thai-Style Chicken, and Alice was practically done with her Beef Portobello. "It must be so neat to have you for a mom," I blurted out.

Alice broke into a big smile, and I felt myself blushing. "Oh, I don't know about that," she said, turning to Emily. "Is it neat to have me as a mom?"

Emily stared at her mother as if she hadn't noticed she was there before. I began to wonder if she had heard the question. Finally, she answered, "I dunno, you're my mom, just a regular mom."

Alice looked disheartened. Then she brightened and said, "Oops, I almost forgot!" She excused herself and after a few minutes I smelled something funny wafting in from the living room. It was an unusual fragrance, something I could not place. Suddenly, it occurred to me it might be marijuana, Mary Jane, cannabis. Pot. I began to panic. Of course it was drugs. After all, didn't Alice joke that she was an old hippie?

Should I call 911? Should I confront her? Or maybe I should just leave. I started to stand up and head to the door when Alice practically knocked me over. She was carrying something that spewed smoke. The smell was so overpowering I thought I would faint.

"I thought you girls might like this," she said, beaming. "I just bought it this afternoon in your honor, Millicent."

Panicked, I looked over at Emily who was rolling her eyes upward. "Not again," she muttered. "Alice, you know I hate that stuff."

"Um, Alice," I tried to gather my strength as she placed the offending object in the middle of the dining room table.

Just say no, I said to myself. *Just say no.*

I braced myself and declared, "In my family we do not smoke marijuana, not even for medicinal purposes."

Alice gave me a funny look. "Nor do we," she said. "It's against the law, you know. However, I hope you have no objection to sandalwood incense."

"That's not marijuana?" I asked, startled.

"Emily!" Alice said as she burst out laughing. "Your friend is so funny. What a great sense of humor!"

Somehow I made it through dinner without suffocating on the incense. Alice and I did most of the talking, and I asked her about her travels and her writing. However, I made sure to modify my questions and comments to sound like a regular eleven-year-old, not someone about to enter her senior year of high school.

Emily did not appear interested at all in the conversation. The minute dinner was over, she grabbed me and we retreated to her room, leaving Alice alone to clear the table.

Emily's room looks like a shrine to adolescent girldom and the complete opposite of my spartan dwelling. Her walls are painted purple and dotted with pink hearts. She has her own phone, stereo system, DVD player, and mini-refrigerator stocked with sodas. Plus, boy-band members who are infinitely more beautiful than I am stare out from posters pledging promises like "I will always love you" and "Hey girl, be mine." Nonetheless, I liked her room.

". . . and look at this," Emily said, flinging open her closet to reveal a white wicker basket full of dirty laundry. "Aren't they the cutest things?" On closer inspection, the laundry turned out to be stuffed animals. "They all won't fit on my bed, so I rotate them so no one will feel left out."

I picked up Shamu, who was resting alongside a threadbare Winnie-the-Pooh. "Did you know that there are lots of whales named Shamu? Shamu was the first killer whale to perform at SeaWorld, and she was so popular that after she died they continued to use her name for all the killer whales."

"Wow, I didn't know that!" Emily looked at Shamu with reverence. "I once heard that they were training killer whales to be lookouts for the Navy. Hey, wanna make jewelry? My dad got me a kit with lots of really neat beads."

Making jewelry was a lot harder and more fun than I had imagined. Emily's necklace had no apparent theme other than bright colors. Carefully, I selected my beads to represent world peace, using a large blue-green bead to signify Earth and several smaller colored beads to depict various countries. In between I threaded a peace symbol and animal beads to illustrate harmony.

Emily alternately read a magazine, danced to pop songs, and

tried to help me string the beads while I completed my master-piece. I was so proud of it when I had finished. "Let me put it on you," Emily offered as she placed it around my neck. "It's beautiful, Millie." I beamed. It was beautiful.

Just as I was admiring my handiwork in the mirror, Emily chirped, "I know! Let's switch, you know, like friendship neck-laces. I'll wear the one you made, and you wear the one I made!"

I hesitated because I loved my necklace so much. But Emily seemed so keen on the idea that suddenly I felt the same way. As the boy-band members looked on, Emily and I exchanged neck-laces and pretended we were being initiated into an elite club in which we were the only members.

That night we stayed up until midnight, and Alice sang the most amusing songs as she accompanied herself on the karaoke machine. One song in particular caught my fancy. It involved an ant who had high hopes about a rubber tree plant. After we sang it a second time, I led an impromptu discussion on the symbol-ism of the ant. Emily and Alice listened intently and later shared their views as we passed around a bowl of popcorn laced with Tabasco sauce. I imagined that this was what Woodstock must have been like.

As I was settling into bed, Emily spoke up. "I am so sorry," she said softly. She looked like an upside-down troll as she hung her head over the top bunk.

"Whatever for?" I asked.

My pillow smelled lemon fresh. I reminded myself to ask Alice what brand of detergent she uses so I can recommend it to my mother. I'm always giving people suggestions on how to improve things. I like to be helpful.

"My mom is so weird," Emily lamented. "I can't believe she forced you to sing with her. And I hate incense. It makes me gag. I think she goes out of her way to embarrass me."

"Really? I thought she was cool." I suppressed the urge to yank Emily's hair.

"You do?"

"Truly."

"Oh Millie, you're the one who's too cool!"

As I shut my eyes, I processed the recent memories of my fine evening. My first sleepover, a friendship necklace, hot Tabasco popcorn, and Emily, who thinks I'm cool.

Yesterday we had a backyard barbecue. While my family ate hot dogs, I was content to munch on grilled corn on the cob, chips dipped in Mom's spicy salsa, and watermelon. Maddie brought over a festive Fourth of July cake that she claimed she made from scratch, but I spied the Butterfield's Bakery box in her car.

It took forever for night to fall. When it finally did, Dad launched several fireworks from our Independence Day Valu-Pak. Simultaneously, I wrote mathematical equations with lit sparklers using the darkness as my blackboard. Maddie and Mom sat in lawn chairs and critiqued our performances by holding up numbers like the Olympic judges. It was so much fun, even though my mother kept giving my dad 10s and throwing kisses to him.

I considered inviting Emily over to the barbecue, but I am still carefully monitoring my parents' behavior. They seem to be doing better these days; however, Dad did chase Mom around the yard, holding two sparklers on the top of his head, pretending to be a bull. If that were not bad enough, Maddie grabbed a tablecloth and whipped it in the air yelling, "Toro, toro, toro!" It's a miracle that I even go out in public with these people.

Family weirdness aside, life is looking up. I have undergone marked improvement in my volleyball game. Coach Gowin actually barked, "All right, Millicent!" when I finally served the ball over the net. The other team was so shocked that they allowed it to fall to the ground unchallenged. I experienced an adrenaline rush that heretofore I had only felt when I aced an exam.

Emily was so proud of me. Afterward, we recounted the serve over and over again. We could have gone on for hours except that when I started to replay my serve for the umpteenth time, Emily was suddenly stricken with a major hangnail. We spent the next half hour debating whether she should clip it off or let it be. It is wonderful how we are always there for each other.

Curiously, Maddie is tickled that Emily and I have bonded. Yesterday, while we were seeing who could stack the most Oreos without making them fall, she kept asking, "Everything okay with you?" the way a person does when they really want to say something else. Finally, Maddie pursed her lips, sighed, then said with a big smile, "Millicent, I am so happy you finally have a friend your age to play with. As much as I love you, I don't think it's healthy for us to spend all our time together."

"I don't mind spending time with you," I comforted her. I

know she must be a little jealous of Emily. "Besides, I don't play. You know that."

At dinner, when Dad mentioned that Emily would be a welcome break from Maddie, a crescent roll slipped from my mother's hand and hit him on the shoulder. "It was an accident," she said, not looking the least bit remorseful.

"So's this," Dad replied, throwing it back at her.

It was just like volleyball practice all over again. I tried to ignore Mom and Dad's antics as I ate. I had a lot on my mind. I am seriously thinking of asking Emily to stay over, but my parents' behavior is troubling.

"Stop!" I finally shouted. Mom and Dad held their crescent rolls up in the air and froze. "This is so childish," I said, lowering my voice just a bit. My mother looked guilty as she bit into her roll and chewed slowly.

"It's all in good fun," my father commented, gently placing his roll back in the bread basket and patting it like a baby.

"Is it?" I asked. "Is it really?"

I went to public school for my elementary education. First through third grades were fine, except for the inane songs we had to sing, usually involving little animals. However, once I hit the fourth grade at age six, my learning curve shot upward while my social curve plummeted into a great abyss. The worst part of my day was recess. That is, until lunchtime when the entire student body descended upon the cafeteria.

"I see London, I see France, I see Betina's underpants!" Digger sang. He was in the second grade, and a year older than me, though he acted much younger.

Seeing the pained look on Betina's face reminded me of the (many) times I had been teased by Digger. If only someone had stood up for me, I thought.

Betina tried to ignore Digger, but he was relentless. I felt so bad for her. Suddenly, I surprised myself by standing up and announcing, "Digger, London is a city, whereas France is a country, so if you knew anything, you'd know that your song is inconsistent." I glanced over to Betina, who was giving me a curious look.

Digger's face turned as red as his hair. He stormed off as Betina and her friends giggled. I had expected her to thank me and perhaps even welcome me into her circle. But it didn't happen. She must have been pretty busy. I'm not sure what exactly is involved with being popular, but it seems to leave you with little time for anyone other than your own kind. Betina and her clique were show-offy girls, the kind that like people to look at them, but then say, "Hey! What are you looking at?" as if they are deeply offended. Still, how difficult would it have been for Betina to say thank you or even acknowledge me?

Later that day I was sitting in my normal spot in the back of the cafeteria with only my chocolate chip cookies for companionship, and they were disappearing fast. From my outpost I could see Betina and company sneaking peeks at Digger. The more they laughed, the redder he got. Then it started.

Digger lobbed a Tater Tot in my direction. "Hey, Mill the Pill, duck!" he shouted. The first one hit my tray and made the girls giggle louder. Before I could deliver a sharp reprimand, I was being bombarded with reconstituted potato bits. As I peered through my fingers, I saw the cafeteria monitor heading toward us with a grimace on her face. Then the next thing I knew, Digger and I were parked outside the principal's office and I noticed that my assailant looked like he was only one chromosome shy of being a serial killer.

"Kill Mill the Pill," Digger whispered to me right before the principal called us into her office. "Digger never forgets kids who double-cross him."

I felt a chill go through me. His threats never bothered me before, but this time was different. As he stared me down, I was suddenly aware of the depth of his spite.

Principal Powell looked stressed. She always looked stressed whenever I saw her, which was often. I liked to report my evaluation of the faculty and the school facilities to her on a biweekly basis. Plus, I was always dropping by her office to keep her informed about the latest education referenda and encouraging her to become more politically active.

Her voice sounded strained and I considered offering her a soothing lozenge, but she was already munching on a handful of

Tums. "Did Digger throw Tater Tots at you, Millicent?" Principal Powell asked.

"No," I said softly with my head bowed.

"Are you sure?" She picked up a pen and started clicking it at an alarming rate. "We have several witnesses, plus you have potato all over your sweater."

I glanced sideways at Digger, who silently mouthed, "Kill Mill the Pill." "I'm sure," I mumbled.

The next day Digger, now joined by his posse of half-witted delinquents, thanked me by flinging chunks of hamburger buns in my direction. This was to be a pattern for the next few months. I didn't mind it so much when it was chips. Digger was too dense to figure out that you can't really throw a potato chip, but that didn't stop him from trying. When he graduated to grapes, though, they really hurt, and I knew I would have to do something to put an end to my mistreatment, even if it meant making a permanent enemy of Digger.

For weeks I deliberated my revenge. Once I hit upon it, it didn't take long to figure out the formula. Timing, though, would be crucial. On the appointed day, I carried my booby-trapped salt shaker into the cafeteria, careful to make sure it remained upright and stable. The cafeteria was serving French fries, and I knew my enemy habitually oversalted.

Digger barely registered any recognition as I sat down, other than to hiss, "Mill the Pill." I rewarded him with a generous smile as I discreetly swapped my salt shaker with the one already on the table. They looked identical, except that mine contained concentrated lemon juice and baking powder, separated by a thin piece of tissue paper.

Right on cue, Digger reached for the salt and began to shake it over his fries. When nothing came out, he kept trying even harder. It was at this point that the tissue broke down and the pressure resulting from the acid-base reaction began to build.

BOOM!!! As planned, the top of the salt shaker flew off amid a shower of foam that covered my tormentor.

As the whole room erupted in laughter, the cafeteria monitor marched straight toward me. It might have been that she had seen the abuse Digger had inflicted on me over the months and figured out who had exacted revenge. Or maybe it was that I had the foresight to bring a Polaroid camera and take pictures. Whatever the reason, I found myself sitting outside Principal Powell's office for the last time.

It's official. Emily will be my first overnight guest! Before I even had the chance to invite her, she suggested it. It's like we are totally in sync. All week I've been prepping my parents on the proper sleepover etiquette:

1. They are to be solicitous, but keep their distance.
2. They are not to discuss politics, kiss, or dance in front of my guest.
3. They are to refrain from mentioning my intellectual achievements or my academic status.

Though Mom and Dad protested, they ultimately agreed to my terms. In return, I promised to put the dirty dishes in the dishwasher instead of in the sink and to stop clipping articles until everyone has had a chance to read the newspaper.

"You should tell her soon," my mother advised as she helped

me tuck my academic citations and certificates into the armoire in the dining room. "Emily will feel betrayed if you don't."

She stopped to catch her breath. Lately, Mom's been unusually tired. When I suggested vitamins, she just said she needs to give up David Letterman. Dad calls her a "Do-It-All." "The only way I can relax is by getting things done," she said, sounding defensive.

"I don't have that problem," Dad chirped from his La-Z-Boy. Neither my mother nor I bothered to respond. It would be like shooting fish in a barrel.

"I'll tell Emily that I'm in high school soon," I assured Mom as I tried to force-fit my chess trophies into the armoire. "Don't worry, I know exactly what I'm doing."

A wing broke off one of the statuettes. I tossed it in with the rest of the awards, figuring there'd be time to glue it back on later.

"Neat house!" Emily enthused.

I was pleased. Our house is neat. I have devised a system of cleaning using charts and graphs to break the house into quadrants and to disseminate assignments. When we all do our part, everything falls into place, except, of course, for large portions of my dad's designated areas.

Oddly, Emily was entranced by my father's den. To make matters worse, he kept dragging out more knickknacks and playthings.

"My dad has the full set of Matchbox cars too," she said. Her eyes got big and she released a huge sigh. "We used to race them together, but now I never see him anymore."

"Oh, well, here's something I'll bet you've never seen." Dad quickly pulled out his Rock'em Sock'em Robots and tried to change the subject. He can't stand it when people are sad. One time when my father saw a barefoot homeless man, he took off his shoes and gave them to him. Then Dad had to run all the way home because it was a really hot day and the sidewalk was sizzling.

"Too cool," Emily said, examining the robots. Immediately, the two of them began boxing.

After a while, I looked at my watch and cleared my throat. "Eh-hem. Dad, Emily is here to socialize with me, not you."

Embarrassed, he excused himself. I detected that Emily was disappointed too. But what was I to do? She was my guest, and though the evening had hardly begun, we were already off schedule.

I was hesitant to show Emily my room. Unlike hers, with her white wrought-iron bunk bed and frilly girl things, my room is functional, albeit small. Aside from the washer and dryer, I have a bed with a sensible blue bedspread that I chose from the JCPenney white sale, a student desk, and lots of bookshelves (which I cleared in anticipation of Emily's visit). As for decorations, the walls used to have plenty of my diplomas, awards, and photos of me shaking hands with important people, but those were in hiding until I could find the right time to tell Emily about my true self. The only thing I didn't take down was my Mona Lisa poster. It's my favorite da Vinci because Mona Lisa looks like she knows more than she's letting on.

To my relief, Emily didn't criticize my decor. Instead, she said, "Wow, you have a washer and dryer in your room? Millie, you are so interesting."

That night, after a delicious dinner (vegetable lasagna, fresh-squeezed lemonade, and Dad's famous double-fudge brownies), we sat on the floor deciding whether or not bangs made Emily's face look round. Impulsively, she pulled my sweater box out from under my bed.

"No!" I cried as I tried to yank it away from her.

"What is it, Millie?" she asked, laughing. "Oooh, some deep dark secret?"

During our ensuing tussle, the box spilled open and my comic book collection scattered all over my room.

I was mortified.

"Millicent Min," Emily declared, "I don't believe it!"

I tried to explain that comics are nothing to be ashamed of, that I keep them for historical reference, when Emily gushed, "I have all of these *Archies* and even some that I don't see here! Don't you just love Betty? I just know that one day she'll win Archie's heart."

We spent the rest of the evening recalling our favorite plot-lines. Oh, how I wish this summer would last forever.

"Millie, we're so alike. It's like we're twins!" Emily proclaimed. "They say that everyone in the world has a twin whether they realize it or not. Isn't it amazing that we've found each other?"

I've always wanted a sibling. However, I suspect my parents were overwhelmed by the challenges of raising a genius. It could not have been easy, either financially or emotionally. My father has yet to recover from the first time I beat him at Monopoly eight years ago. To this day he insists that had he not landed in jail, Marvin Gardens would have been his.

My guest and I were trying to have a decent conversation about which was better, peds or tube socks, but my mother kept coming into my room to check the dryer and say inane things like, "If you don't take cottons out at the exact right moment, they wrinkle and you have to iron them."

"Here, let me help you," Emily said, leaping up and waving her fingertips in the air.

I have boxes of nail polish and beads and girlish things my grandparents in Arizona send me for birthdays and Christmas. They live in a condo on a golf course and don't know what to make of me. I think I scare them.

Emily had painted her fingernails using a palette of red, maroon, and orange and then overlapped various hues on her toenails. I was reminded of the work of the artist Mark Rothko. After much deliberation, I selected a tasteful shade of peach. My right hand looked fine, but the other hand looked like I had a monkey for a manicurist. I am a lefty, but consider myself in good company. Famous left-handers include Pablo Picasso, Eudora Welty, Harry Truman, and Oprah Winfrey.

My mother smiled as she filled the laundry basket with clothes fresh from the dryer. She held Dad's tattered Hang Ten T-shirt against her face. She loves it when the laundry is still warm. Once I caught her sitting under just-dried sheets reading a book.

"That's all right, Emily," Mom said, leaning against the dryer to steady herself. "This is the last load. I'll leave you girls alone now."

I mouthed "thank you" to my mother. She winked and shut the door.

"Wow," Emily said as she blew on her nails. "I wish I had a family like yours. Your parents are so normal."

Normal? My parents? It's common knowledge that fumes from nail polish can affect your brain and cause you to hallucinate. I opened my bedroom window to let in some fresh air as Emily and I read aloud from my comics. Since she was the guest, Emily got to be Archie and I was Jughead. We took turns being Betty and Veronica. It was hysterical. We laughed so hard that after a while no sound came out, and we were too delirious to even turn another page.

My father is in pain and lying flat on his back on the floor. He says it is all Maddie's fault. Maddie says he needs more exercise.

My grandmother called earlier today to tell us she was coming over with big news. I was certain she was finally getting a shar-pei puppy, since she has been talking about it forever. However, she has chosen to make an even more life-altering change.

About six months ago, not long after my grandfather died, Maddie decided she needed something new to occupy her time. She narrowed it down to feng shui or real estate and then consulted the tea leaves. Both appealed to her because, as she put it, "People actually pay you to poke around their homes and tell them what to do."

"To think, all these years she's been doing that for free," Dad whispered to Mom.

"I heard that, Jack," Maddie informed him. She has a keen sense of hearing and claims to have once heard a bubble burst.

The tea leaves said she should become a feng shui master. In her words, she will "be a conduit in the six-thousand-year-old Chinese art of balancing wind over water to create harmonious environments." (She's going to tell people where to move their furniture.) Hence the huge wooden dragon she bought on my last day of school. Originally he resided in the kitchen, but every time I visit, he's in another room. She has named the dragon Julius.

"After Julius Caesar?" I asked.

"No, after Orange Julius," she replied. It is her second-favorite drink. Green tea is number one.

Though we usually converse in English, Maddie is now insisting on speaking Chinese. She believes people will pay more if they think she's an authentic feng shui master. She's learning conversational Cantonese via a series of audiotapes she bought from the Home Shopping Network. Unfortunately, Maddie's Chinese accent sounds more Chilean to me.

Tonight, before her announcement, Maddie practiced feng shui on our living room and made Dad change the furniture into several different configurations, finally selecting one that was not that far off from where they began. I thought my father was going to kill her, which is totally against the "positive flow of chi" that Maddie was striving for.

After my father collapsed on the floor, Maddie called a Min Family Meeting. When I started to recite the bylaws forbidding non-Mins, both my parents gave me "that look." Their precision timing was very impressive. I wonder if they practice.

I clamped my mouth shut as we gathered around Dad, who was still lying on the floor in the living room. He kept glaring at Maddie and muttering, but he couldn't move. Maddie began, "You know, when I was younger I always wanted to join the Peace Corps. . . ."

"You're joining the Peace Corps?" I yelped. Maddie cannot even stand it when bathrooms have those hand dryers instead of paper towels. How could she make it in the Peace Corps?

"Millicent," Maddie said sharply, "for once would you let someone finish their thought before analyzing it? I said I *wanted* to join the Peace Corps. Of course that would be silly now, but the urge to travel is still in my system. . . ."

Maddie has always been an armchair traveler. My grandparents had talked of going to Europe for their sapphire anniversary before Grandpa got sick. It's amazing. One night you go to bed all happy because you just won an essay contest on global warming, then when you wake up in the morning, your mother's sitting on the edge of your bed telling you that your grandfather is dying.

"Grandpa and I always wanted to see the world." Maddie continued to pace, careful not to step on Dad. "But we never took the time to do it. So now that's what we're going to do."

Mom and Dad looked at each other.

"But Maddie," I hastened to tell her, "Grandpa died, remember?" My mother bit her lip, and Dad gripped her hand.

"Yes, gone," she said, saddened for a moment. She quickly perked up and added, "But not forgotten." Maddie held up a pendant she was wearing around her neck. It looked like a small vase. "His ashes," she said reverently. "Some of his ashes are in here. Now we can travel two for the price of one!"

Maddie has decided to enroll in the London branch of Fenwick & Feldie's Feng Shui Academy. After that, she plans to tour Europe "until they kick me out or the money dries up, whatever comes first."

I must have looked stricken. "Oh, Millicent," Maddie said, giving me a hug. "Sometimes I think you would really do yourself a favor if you learned not to take everything so seriously."

But this was serious business. My grandmother was taking my grandfather's ashes on a tour of Europe? I'm afraid the rest of the world isn't ready for Maddie.

Stanford aside, everything was practically perfect until Maddie dropped her bombshell. My poetry class is humming along and so is my relationship with Emily. You couldn't ask for a better friend. We see or phone each other daily and have never run out of things to say, except for that one time when Maddie forced her kiwi–peanut butter scones on us. I spit mine out, but Emily ate hers and somehow managed to smile at the same time. She's really an amazing person.

Oh sure, Emily has a few flaws. But don't we all. For example, I am lax about cleaning out my three-hole punch. As for Emily, there are a few things about her that drive me nuts. Like the way she's always feigning interest in whatever my dad's latest hobby is. Or how she insists on helping my mom around the house, which is ludicrous since she never lifts a finger at her own house. And then there are the boys. Emily is boy crazy.

I consider boys a huge waste of time. Emily argues that they are what life's all about and is prone to swooning whenever she sees a cute one. I am far more interested in getting my degree than fawning over something as inconsequential as a boy. But I can't tell her that. She still thinks I'm in middle school.

Shortly after "The Incident," as the Digger/Salt Shaker Debacle has come to be known in our family, we attempted homeschooling. Since my mother had a 9-to-5 job, or in her case an 8-to-6:30, the burden fell upon my father, who was in between contracts. We were both excited about the prospect of getting to know each other better and sharing our insights.

That said, after many arguments, numerous threats from both sides of the table, and several genuine attempts at détente, Dad and I met my mother at the door. We did not even allow her the courtesy of putting the grocery bags down before we simultaneously launched into our separate versions of events.

"I don't understand," Mom said, looking worried. "You quit? You both quit?" My father and I nodded. "But it's only been one day," she continued as we trailed her into the kitchen. "Don't you think you ought to give it more of a chance?" In unison, Dad and I shook our heads.

The next thing I know, I'm taking a tour of Star Brite.

"If everyone here is so bright, why is the name spelled wrong?" I asked.

"Shhhh," Mom nudged me in the side. She's always shushing or nudging my father and me. "There is such a thing as being too smart."

Star Brite was happy to take me. "It would be an honor," Dr. Marks said, "to educate a young person as brilliant as Millicent." He bent over so we were eye to eye and patted me on the head. "Millicent is exactly the sort of student who excels at Star Brite. I just know we are going to be pals, aren't we, Millie?" I just stared at him until he sputtered, "Ahem, okay! Well then, let me give you a VIP tour of your new school."

That night I tried on my school uniform. It included a starched white shirt under a precision-pleated navy plaid jumper made of rash-inducing polyester. The hem of the jumper almost reached my ankles before Mom hemmed it up. Still, it was far too big and made me look as if I were shrinking.

Emily is excited about going to school in Rancho Rosetta. "I'll bet the guys here are cuter than the ones in New Jersey," she declared as she scoped out the boys at the mall.

"I wouldn't know," I murmured. I was adding up our Taco Bell receipt to make sure we hadn't been overcharged. Before I had a chance to tally the tax, Emily got up and pulled me over to the photo booth.

"C'mon Millie, we gotta do this!" We crammed inside and took two series of photos, one for each of us. I don't think I've ever laughed so hard when getting my picture taken. Most of the time Dad frowns and yells out, "Millicent, at least pretend to be having a good time."

All my life my parents have been obsessed with my having a good time. When I was younger, they enrolled me in Tumbling Tots, forced me to take finger-painting lessons, and even purchased an annual pass to the Rancho Rosetta Children's Theater with the hopes that I might be smitten by the colorful costumed characters on the stage. Mom and Dad even bought me Sea Monkeys, a Mr. Potato Head, and a kite shaped like a butterfly. Luckily, my father likes all those toys, so they haven't gone to waste.

What my parents kept failing to understand was how happy I was when I was alone with my books. There was no pressure to perform or be cute, and books never disappoint — unless, of course, you've chosen a bad one. But then, you can always put it down and pick up another one without any repercussions.

Last Thursday, we had a close call. Stanford had been his usual goonie self during our tutoring/torture session. Oooh, he makes me so mad! Since he showed no interest in his mandatory book reports, Mrs. Martinez and I selected three novels for him.

From the Mixed-up Files of Mrs. Basil E. Frankweiler is about two kids who hide out in a museum for several days and solve a mystery. I remembered reading it when I was three and wanting to do the same.

Holes I chose because I like to imagine that Stanford is one of the boys at the hideous detention camp set out in the middle of nowhere.

I thought *Number the Stars* would be good because it teaches history and questions the meaning of life. I first read it when I was five and reread it again recently. I like to reread books after letting a significant amount of time pass. You can't imagine what went through my mind when I first read Truman Capote's *In Cold Blood* when I was six. I couldn't sleep for weeks. When I read it again last year, I couldn't sleep for days. I take that as a sign that I've matured.

"Wake up," I hissed at Stanford. "We have to go over the parts of speech again. Here, I've made a list for you with examples. Plus, you should be up to at least chapter six in *From the Mixed-up Files of Mrs. Basil E. Frankweiler* and ready to discuss it."

"No fair!" Stanford groaned. I don't know what's not fair about keeping up with homework assignments. Apparently, Stanford thinks that teachers and tutors were put on this Earth to antagonize him, when actually it is the other way around.

"Sit up," I ordered as I handed him the list. It included:

NOUN: A person, place, thing, or idea. *The brilliant* <u>tutor</u> *tried to teach the ignorant boy.*

ADJECTIVE: A word that describes a noun. *The* <u>pea-brained</u> *basketball player did not even attempt to study.*

VERB: A word that expresses an action. *The police <u>arrested</u> him and threw him in jail.*

ADVERB: A word used to describe a verb or adjective. *The boy apologized <u>profusely</u>, but it was too late and he was fed to the wolves.*

I spent the rest of the session lecturing Stanford on proper study habits. When I was done, I was met with total silence.

There are good silences, like the beat after a fabulous play has just ended and before the audience jumps to its feet applauding. Then there are bad silences, like after you've said, "Actually, the hypotenuse is 3.4 centimeters off" to your father's supervisor. Stanford's silence created a new category: the infinite silence of limbo where your words are released into the atmosphere but mysteriously disappear before they reach their target.

As Stanford and I exited the library, we hit the invisible fork in the road. He went left, I went right, and neither of us said good-bye. I was eager to meet up with Emily since we both had errands to take care of. She was running dangerously low on Stellar Strawberry Bonne Bell LipSmackers, and I was in dire need of lead for my mechanical pencils.

So there we were, waiting in line at the drugstore when Emily starts tugging on my T-shirt. It was really annoying because I had just ironed it that morning. "That boy's looking at you, Millie," she whispered as she brushed the cookie crumbs off the front of her dress.

I looked up, and to my horror Stanford was in the next line gripping a tube of Clearasil. Upon making eye contact, we both quickly turned away.

"Millie, you're all red. Do you know him?" Emily asked. I could not believe she was smiling at him. "Is he from around here? Oh, he's soooo dreamy."

"Looks like a nightmare to me," I muttered as I watched Stanford ditch the pimple cream and scurry out the emergency exit.

As we sat at the kitchen table, I watched my mother with morbid fascination as she ate an entire banana cream pie, minus my meager slice. I was telling her about Professor Skylanski's insightful interpretation of Emerson's "The Rhodora." My account must have been so mesmerizing that she didn't realize how much she had eaten. When finished, Mom looked down and said with surprise, "Oh my. Did I do that?"

My poetry class is going exceedingly well, as is my camaraderie with Emily. To this day we both still wear the friendship necklaces we made at our first sleepover. She keeps hers on 24/7, and I only take mine off when I shower. I've even programmed her phone number into #4 on our speed dial. (#1 is Maddie, #2 is Mom's office, #3 is Pizza Wheels.)

At volleyball yesterday, Julie tried to be mean to us again, but Emily wouldn't allow it.

". . . It's not like jumping is such a hard thing to do," Julie chided us. (Both Emily and I are earthbound when it comes to blocking the ball.) "Even a little kid knows how to jump."

"Well, maybe you could stay late and teach us how to jump," Emily suggested, giving me a wink. I couldn't help but add, "Yes, Julie, you say jump and we'll ask 'how high' and then you can demonstrate for us."

Julie tried to figure out if we were making fun of her or actually asking for her help. Not that she'd give us any. With her, it's like a battle, only no one has formally declared war.

On the topic of war, here is my list for some of the greatest battles in recent history:

1. Gary Kasparov vs. Deep Blue
2. Muhammad Ali vs. Joe Frazier
3. Millicent Min vs. Stanford Wong

It is one thing to be against a worthy opponent where logic and wits prevail. But to be pitted against someone who is oblivious is maddening. It's like trying to shoot a falling leaf with a cannon. Even though I bring years of literary insight, the patience of a paleontologist, and plenty of Peanut M&M's to my task, Stanford adopts a defiant attitude that I cannot penetrate. "Just try," I plead. "Just give the books a chance. Would that be so hard?"

Mrs. Wong offered me a fifty-dollar bonus if Stanford passes his class. Not that I ever expect to see it. Stanford plows through a book about as fast as a cataract patient reading an eye chart. He claims that reading zaps his energy for important things like basketball.

When people talk I can block them out. I let my mind go as their mouths move and their hands wave about. I can always tell when they are winding down because they look at me as if they expect me to agree with them. That's when I tune back into the conversation and make the appropriate noises like "Yes, yes, I think you have a point there," or "That sounds reasonable." I have found that these two phrases work for most situations.

With Stanford I have been forced to develop a third phrase: "I don't believe you." He comes up with the most elaborate excuses for not completing his assignments. One even involved a brown dog, a skateboard, and the FedEx man. I have never failed at anything academic before. However, Stanford Wong may break my record.

Today he had his nose buried in *Number the Stars*. I heard him gurgle and gag, then realized he had fallen asleep and was drooling!

"Who was that girl you were with?" he asked after I kicked him under the table several times in an effort to wake him.

"What girl?"

Stanford rubbed his leg. "At the drugstore the other day."

"No one you know."

"She seemed nice," he mused. "What's her name?"

"Emily," I said, revealing more than I wanted to.

"Did she ask about me?" he asked, showing more interest in the chance encounter with Emily than in all of our tutoring sessions combined.

"No," I lied. "Though we did laugh when you set off the emergency alarm."

Stanford looked dejected, and for a moment I almost regretted what I had said. Still, he was taking an irritating interest in Emily, and she was my friend, not his.

Suddenly, Stanford sat up, as if he had a great epiphany. "Hey, that Emily seemed pretty cool. What's she doing hanging around with a nerdling like you?"

"Better me than you," I snapped.

"Maybe you could introduce us," he ventured.

"Maybe not," I told him.

The thought of Stanford meeting Emily made me panic. If they ever met it was a sure thing he'd spill the beans about my academic status.

I flashed back to the other day when I had been tempted to tell Emily the truth about my alter ego: Millicent L. Min, College Coed. However, I'm afraid that if she learns I went through middle school while she was still getting hooked on phonics, she might treat me differently. Not that she would ever call me a nerdling, like Stanford. Or use me like Debbie. Still, it could change everything. For her sake, I'm electing not to tell her the truth for a little while longer. What can it hurt?

Stanford leaned forward. "Hey, Millicent," he said in a whisper, only it was still pretty loud since his volume control is broken. "Remember, you promised not to tell anyone you're tutoring me, right? I mean, if that girl or the guys at basketball ever find out, it could ruin my reputation."

I wondered what kind of reputation he had, and how much lower it could possibly go. "Well," I said, pretending to think about it. "I guess if it's so important to you then I won't."

Stanford looked relieved. "Thanks, Millicent, that's really decent of you."

My stomach felt funny as I gave him a weak smile and continued with the day's lesson.

Last night, Emily and I had a huge argument over the definition of "attractive." She seems to think it has a lot to do with good hair, sparkling eyes, and the ability to make a person melt. Me, I believe that it encompasses the ability to communicate (the written word, as well as spoken), high intelligence, and a firm grasp of current events.

As I pulled out my *Webster's* and proceeded to defend my position, Emily playfully grabbed it and tossed it across the room, hitting Mona Lisa on the face. "I want to know what *you* think, Millie," she said. "Not some dumb dictionary."

I could not believe her nerve. *Merriam-Webster's Dictionary* is a great reference, scholarly and highly entertaining. I have spent countless hours in my tree perusing it.

"Hey! Watch where you throw that," I said as I retrieved my dictionary and checked Mona Lisa for signs of injury. She was still smiling. "If you really want to know what I think attractive means, then I'll make a list. . . ."

"A list!" she exclaimed. "Yes, let's both make a list, but instead of 'attractive,' I've got a better idea."

TOP 10 LIST OF ATTRIBUTES FOR THE IDEAL HUSBAND

Emily	Millie
1. Sparkling eyes	1. High IQ
2. Good hair	2. Interest in world affairs
3. Rich	3. Well read
4. Nice car	4. Excellent domestic skills
5. Fun	5. Appreciation of art
6. Athletic	6. Nonsmoker
7. Romantic	7. Good hygiene
8. Loyal	8. Clean driving record
9. Strong	9. Love of travel
10. Good dancer	10. Graduate degree

"Do you think I'm attractive?" I asked my mother after Emily went home. She was clipping coupons and then filing them into the accordion organizer that accompanies her to the grocery store.

"Of course you are," she said as she expertly trimmed a baking soda coupon. She believes that baking soda can clean practically anything. "You are very attractive."

My mother was homecoming queen when she went to JFK

High School. It made sense. Unlike me, she's highly photogenic and would look good in a crown. What's curious is that I never knew she was queen until I overheard her telling Emily one day while they were folding towels. I wonder what other information she has kept from me?

It has not gone unnoticed that Mom and Emily are developing a close camaraderie. They talk fashion and skin care, and have found their equals when it comes to shopping, though each has a different approach to the sport. Mom shops sales to see how much she can save. Emily rings up her father's Visa card to see how much she can spend. Nonetheless, both possess the kind of stamina usually reserved for top athletes. They also share a dream to visit the 4.2 million-square-foot Mall of America in Bloomington, Minnesota.

I wouldn't call Emily spoiled. Yet who ever heard of a twelve-year-old with her own credit card? Her father gave it to her for emergencies. To Emily walking into a store constitutes an emergency. She is always flaunting her Visa and saying loudly, "I'd like to charge that to my *father's* account." Or "I just know my *father* would want me to have this."

No one has ever questioned her or even asked to see any ID. Once she gets home she just throws her purchases into her closet, bag and all. I am not sure if Alice is even aware of this. Then again, I get the feeling that Alice and Emily don't talk much. Personally, I love talking with Alice. She's always telling me about the books she just read, or floating ideas by me for future articles. I feel that she takes me seriously, even if Emily believes that her mom has been put on this Earth to annoy her. A lot of our conversations begin, "You won't believe what Alice said to me this time. . . ."

I don't know why Emily is always so mad at her mother. If Alice were my mom, I'd want to tell her everything.

Stanford was in such a hurry to get out of tutoring and on with basketball that he left his books behind. I knew that he had a quiz coming up so, against my better judgment, I decided to return his books to him.

As I approached the park, I could see Stanford Wong, barbaric buffoon, playing basketball with a bunch of other boys. What I observed was shocking. Even though he wasn't the biggest or the tallest, it was clear he was the one in charge. A group of girls stood off to the side, pretending not to watch him. When he saw me, he missed his shot and made a sour face.

"Stanford, I need to see you for a minute," I informed him. I wondered if he felt as awkward as I did with everyone staring at us.

"Can't it wait?" he said, lowering his voice and hardly moving his lips.

"No," I said.

He released a huge sigh. "Gotta go," Stanford mumbled as he rushed me away from his friends.

The girls looked at me with curious, envious eyes. A gawky carrot-topped boy stood with his hands on his hips. He looked familiar. "Hey Stanford, come back, we're not finished yet."

"No, I gotta go," Stanford snapped. He walked so fast I had to run to keep up with him.

"Forget her, let's play," the redheaded boy insisted. I could feel him glaring at me. "Stanford, come back. We need you!"

It had never occurred to me that Stanford might be popular or that he had any real athletic talent or friends. To me he had always been the imbecile that Maddie thrust upon me. And now here he was in all his glory, King of the Sierra Vista Playground.

"Don't talk to me," Stanford hissed as I tried to catch up to him. "I don't want to be seen with you. What are you doing here?"

"Your books," I said, handing them to him. "You've got a quiz tomorrow in your English class."

Stanford stopped and faced me. "Yeah, well . . ." he said, taking the offending objects. "Thanks, I guess."

I thought I was doing something nice. But nice isn't always reciprocated. I recall that back at Star Brite, when I learned the others only ate lunch with me for bonus points, I was admittedly a bit depressed.

"You just need to learn how to mingle," my father said.

"Once kids get to know the real Millicent, they can't help but love you."

Spoken like a true father.

Dad slid a brown paper bag across the kitchen table. Inside was a box of Moon Pies. "Pass these out on the playground," he whispered as if the Moon Pie Police might intervene. "I guarantee you'll be the most popular kid out there."

"Daaaad," I began to protest.

"Promise me you'll try." He looked so sincere, I was afraid of hurting his feelings. My father's a sensitive male.

"I'll try," I sighed, taking the bag.

Sure enough, Dad was right. I was a hit. For all of about seventeen seconds. Once the Moon Pies were gone, my popularity polls plummeted. A couple of the girls had managed to say, "Thank you, Maggie," but that was as close to a lasting relationship as I came.

So there I was. Just some little kid standing on the playground with an empty box of Moon Pies. A sudden gust of wind began to blow the wrappers away and I ran after them, lest they add "litterer" to my résumé, which already included "outcast" and "egghead." When I was done I sat on an empty bench. Luckily, I had slipped a Moon Pie in my pocket. It was all smashed but I ate it anyway.

"Um, I'd better get back to the game," Stanford said. He was looking at me funny. "Are you okay, Millie?"

I looked around and instead of an empty playground, I was surprised to find myself in a park full of kids.

"Yes, yes, I'm fine," I assured him. "Hey, good luck on your quiz tomorrow."

"Right," he replied, sounding dejected. "Like I'm really going to pass."

"You might," I said. "You're not as stupid as I first thought you were."

"Gee thanks, Mill, and you're not as big a blockhead as I thought you were," Stanford answered.

I almost smiled, but caught myself just in time.

I love Emily, but she can be so superficial. She just devours those insipid fashion magazines as if they were malted milk balls.

"Oooh, look at her," gushed Emily as she pointed to an emaciated waif. At first I thought the sad-faced girl was a starving refugee. Then Emily explained that "Patka" was a highly compensated supermodel who had aspirations of becoming a doctor and curing the world of acne.

I took a second look and indeed, Patka was sheathed in a designer faux-distressed ensemble.

"That girl has an eating disorder. Her bones are deteriorating and she will live to regret the decisions of her youth." I sniffed as I turned the pages of Emily's latest *Archie* comic.

"Well," Emily said, "you're assuming that's her real body. I think a lot of the magazines alter the bodies on the computer. No one really looks like that. Anyway, real or not, look at her marvelous outfit. We have to go to the mall. That skirt is so cute. I just know my dad would want me to have that skirt."

I wanted to tell her that maybe a mini wasn't the most flattering thing for her figure. But then, Emily is funny about her weight. She doesn't consider herself heavy. "I'm big-boned," she's told me more than once. "Why's everyone so concerned with my weight if I'm not? And honestly, Millie, don't you think you could stand to gain a few pounds? Then maybe you wouldn't always have to wear that ugly green belt to hold up your pants."

I ignored her pants comment. It's true that I have to wear a belt, but the belt is far from ugly. It used to be my grandfather's and it practically wraps around my waist twice. Dad had to punch several more holes into it to make it fit. Still, I would not trade it for anything.

As we read in silence, I savored the camaraderie. Here we were, just two regular friends reading side by side, when all of a sudden, Emily shouted, "Look! A quiz. I love these quizzes." I looked up just as Reggie was about to trip Jughead. I love quizzes too. "Let's take the quiz," she pleaded. "Come on, please!!!!"

"Sure, why not?" I was glad it was something else we could do together. I had no idea Emily would enjoy a quiz. Perhaps I had misjudged her. Every day we're learning new things about each other. Plus, I was in the mood for a quiz.

Earlier, Stanford had been waiting for me outside the library. "I passed!" he said, all smiles. "I actually passed!"

He got a C-plus on his quiz, but this didn't seem to bother him. In fact, he was proud. I would have been mortified to get a grade lower than an A-minus.

"Let the quiz begin," I said to Emily. "But I ought to warn you, I'm really good at this sort of stuff!"

"Okay," Emily said, grabbing a pen off my desk and removing the cap with her teeth. "Question number one: If you were invited to a 1960s theme party, would you: A) get reacquainted with Mary Quant; B) rim your eyes in black kohl; C) dig out your fishnets and go-go boots; or D) all of the above?"

It was a stupid quiz. I could not believe I even consented to take it. After we had tallied our scores Emily tried to console me. "You're just upset because you didn't do too well," she said. "But that's okay, it was pretty dumb."

YOUR FASHION HIGH-Q RESULTS
Score <u>4</u> out of 25 — Try, try again. Sorry,
but you need to go back to fashion school.
Study up on the trends, get hot tips
from your friends, be bold and experiment,
and get ready for next month's exciting
Fashion High-Q Quiz!

Not only did I not do well, I failed the Fashion High-Q Quiz.

I'm not sure if the other girls on the volleyball team put up with me because I am Emily's friend or because they genuinely don't despise me. No one's calling me names anymore, and Julie almost smiled at me once. Emily says, "It's more work to be mean than it is to be nice." Sometimes she's pretty perceptive.

"Lights out," my mother said through the closed door. Emily snuggled into her sleeping bag and then brought out a beat-up old stuffed animal.

"What is that thing?" I asked.

"My bear," she said defensively. "His name is TB. That's short for Teddy Bear. My dad gave him to me when I was little. It's TB's turn to sleep with me tonight." Emily held him up so I could see. He looked like something you'd find on the side of the road.

"Are you aware that TB also stands for tuberculosis?" I asked.

"TB is always here for me when I need him," she went on as

she adjusted his nose, which was smashed to one side. "Who do you turn to when you're lonely? Do you have a favorite stuffed animal? Everyone needs a favorite stuffed animal."

I have never allowed for invisible friends or any of those classic childhood fabrications. I tried to keep an open mind about Santa when I saw how important he was to the adults in my life. Yet when faced with the mathematical improbability of his delivering so many gifts in a mere twelve-hour period, I just could not see how it could be so.

Before I could answer Emily's question, Mom knocked on the door again. "Come in!" Emily called out.

My mother stuck her head into the room. "Just wanted to say good night," she started saying. She stopped when she spotted TB. "Oooh, look at this adorable bear," she said, kneeling down to give him a hug. Emily beamed. How could Mom even tell he was a bear? "You know, I used to sleep with a stuffed animal when I was your age," Mom said, looking wistful. "A funny little dog who I'd whisper my secrets to before I went to sleep. I'm not sure what happened to him."

When my mother closed the door, Emily asked again, "So, Millie, who do you turn to when you get lonely?"

lone·ly \ˈlōn-lē\ *adj* lone·li·er; -est (1607) **1 a** : being without company : LONE **b** : cut off from others :

SOLITARY   **2** : not frequented by human beings : DESOLATE
3 : sad from being alone : LONESOME   **4** : producing a
feeling of bleakness or desolation   *syn* see ALONE

I gave it some thought. True, I have led a somewhat solitary
life and have on rare occasion wondered what it would be like to
be popular. But it is not as if I sat alone in my room all day
brooding. My life was so full with my studies and endless projects that there really wasn't time for friendships. And if there
wasn't time for friendships, then wouldn't it follow that there
wasn't time for loneliness? As it was, I had put cryptarithms (my
favorite form of math puzzle) and other things on hold to make
room for Emily.

I turned off my reading lamp. "I don't get lonely," I answered.
Was my voice wavering, I wondered?

Okay, it is possible I have experienced small aches once or
twice when observing kids at school running up to their friends
and sharing secrets. And from time to time, I wondered what it
might be like to have someone to walk to class with or to call
when something great has happened. Someone in my own gen-
eration, that is. Now that I finally have a best friend, I can understand why Maddie is so lonely sometimes. Grandpa was more
than her husband. He was her friend.

It was like one day my grandfather is healthy and organizing
a protest, and the next day he's sick in the hospital. My grand-

father took a long four months to die, even though the doctors only gave him two. Maddie says he was never one for listening to authority figures.

"How are you doing in school?" he'd ask. "Keep up the good grades and you're sure to be valedictorian." The tubes and wires plugged into him made him resemble some sort of bionic man, only he didn't look invincible. "Wow, valedictorian," he wheezed. "That would sure be something. I'd like to see my little Millie knock the socks off of those big kids."

Grandpa never finished high school. It was his only regret, he said.

"I'll do my best," I promised as I reviewed his medical chart.

"He's a fighter," Maddie whispered proudly as Grandpa slept. He looked so weak and tired. I hoped that whatever he was fighting for was worth it.

My grandfather's funeral was strange. Lots of people got up and told stories, and there was laughing and crying going on at the same time. Some of the policemen who had arrested him for protesting over the years were there. Even Stanford and his family came to pay their last respects. It was the only time Stanford and I didn't greet each other with insults. He came over to me on his own and mumbled, "I'm sorry, Millie, your grandfather was so cool." Then he walked away without even saying anything about my crying.

After the funeral, our living room was full of people I didn't know consoling Maddie and Mom. It was boring and disconcerting, so I slipped away. But even if I had jumped up and down and shouted, "I'm leaving now!" no one would have noticed.

I stayed in my tree until night began to fall. The street was lined with cars I did not recognize. It was quiet, except for the low murmurs of people consoling Maddie. Through my binoculars, I could barely make out Max across the street in an army costume, hiding among the blue hydrangea bushes. An empty paper towel tube doubled as his telescope.

All of a sudden, Max's parents scurried out of their house, jumped into the station wagon, and took off. Bewildered, Max stepped out into the deserted driveway. Just then, the car came to a screeching halt and then slowly reversed. Max was scooped up and the station wagon disappeared into the darkness.

When no one came to get me, I went back inside. The crowd was gone. Maddie, Mom, and Dad sat on the couch like zombies. They hadn't even bothered turning on the lights. There was no dinner on the table, and I was starving. So I ordered an extra large pizza — the veggie special without onions, the way Grandpa and I liked it. I kept thinking about how we used to argue over who'd get the slice with the most mushrooms. By the time it arrived, I wasn't hungry anymore.

As I stared at the giant pizza, I never felt lonelier in my life.

Without warning, *THUMP*! A pillow hit me over the head. Emily laughed her big, throaty laugh. "Earth to Millie, Earth to

Millie," she shouted. I looked up, surprised to find her poised to strike me again.

"Hey!" I said. I picked up my pillow and swatted her with such ferocity that she fell over backward. She didn't move and for a moment I was afraid I had killed her. Then I heard her chortle. It started softly and rose to fill the room.

"Ooooh, you are in so much trouble," Emily shrieked as she proceeded to pummel me with her pillow. I took the defensive and whacked her back repeatedly. She was a fierce opponent. I'm not sure whose pillow burst first, mine or hers, but soon my room resembled a snowstorm. The door opened, and Emily and I froze as feathers swirled around us.

Mom's jaw dropped, and Dad's eyes bugged out. Neither spoke.

"I am so sorry," Emily said, bowing her head so she wouldn't start giggling.

"Me too," I said.

But I really wasn't.

July 25

My father was acting strange all morning. Stranger than usual, that is. He had even combed his hair and used some of Mom's mousse to give it the oomph, shine, and unsurpassed hold favored by Hollywood hairstylists. Mom was acting funny too. I think they were having one of their fights.

Dad had an important interview today. That's why he was wearing the suit he had bought for Grandpa's funeral. He looked as uncomfortable in it this morning as the day we buried my grandfather.

"Do I have to go?" I overheard Dad asking Mom. My stethoscope comes in very handy at times like these.

"Yes," she said firmly. "We've talked about this before and now more than ever you need a job." There was a long silence. Then Mom let loose one of her famous sighs. "Jack, things are going to change around here, and there's no ignoring it."

It all sounded so clear. I was amazed at what my stethoscope could pick up.

"Millie," my father said. He sounded like he was right next to me. I could practically hear him breathing. "It's time for breakfast." He placed his hand on my shoulder. "Please put the stethoscope away."

Despite Mom's renowned Smiley Face French Toast, Dad moped all through breakfast. To cheer him up, I offered to practice shaking hands with him, but he was too despondent to even respond. As it was, he blindly ate the French toast, not even noticing the beatific banana smile and googly blueberry eyeballs.

I know why he has to get a job. It's that money thing again. I guess Mom's tired of being the main contributor to the Min family bottom line. She's not been herself lately. I saw her watching *Terms of Endearment* on television last night. The film features a turbulent mother–daughter relationship that is reconciled right before the daughter dies. Mom cried through the whole movie, even the commercials.

At least I am earning some money this summer, torture that it is. This afternoon I called a parent conference with Mrs. Wong. We agreed to meet at Stout's, the coffee shop famous for its homemade pies.

Mrs. Wong showed up right on time, looking like she had an appointment with the head of a Fortune 500 company, not the eleven-year-old tutor of her son. Then again, Mrs. Wong has impeccable manners and treats me like a grown-up. It is hard to believe this elegant, sophisticated woman is the mother of Noodle Brain.

"Stanford doesn't tell me anything about how the tutoring is going," she said, adjusting her necklace. I suspect it's a real diamond. Maddie says that the Wongs have money. "Millicent, how do you think it's going?" She leaned in, eager for my assessment.

My mouth was full of french silk pie. As I put down my fork, I pondered how to explain to Mrs. Wong that her son is a foul-smelling ignoramus without hurting her feelings. "He's impossible, a putrid dimwit, a dunce with the manners of a primate," I wanted to say. Instead, I remembered my upbringing and that my mother threatened to take away my PBS privileges if I slandered Stanford.

"It's been hard," I told Mrs. Wong haltingly. "Stanford barely knows the minimum to get by, like on his quizzes. He just doesn't seem motivated."

"That's not surprising," she replied. She hadn't touched her coffee or her jumbleberry pie. "The only thing that seems to motivate Stanford these days is basketball."

After much discussion, Mrs. Wong and I decided that an extra half hour a day of reading *before* any basketball might be just the thing Stanford needed to "encourage" his studies.

Mrs. Wong explained that last year Stanford cut English to play basketball, which is why he did not pass. "Of course," she added, as she paid the check, "I'm sure cutting school is something you would know nothing about."

"So true," I responded, laughing along with her. I hoped my pupils weren't dilating as people's sometimes do when they are lying.

There was a time when I did have a slight truancy problem, though it's not as if I were a delinquent or anything. I had adult supervision. It was during the period when Digger was using me for target practice. Rather than subject myself to his lunchtime abuse, I'd sometimes feign illness, especially on days when the cafeteria was serving hard food like crispy chicken nuggets or teriyaki beef bites.

My modus operandi generally went like this:

1. Roll around bed — clutch stomach and moan lightly
2. Take thermometer from Mom
3. Feign dehydration, request water
4. When Mom leaves the room, stick thermometer against the light bulb until it reaches 100.5 degrees (hot enough to stay home, not hot enough for medication or a doctor's visit)

Then a call would be placed to Maddie, and she'd come over and we'd eat frozen Milky Ways, play two-handed bridge, and go through Mom and Dad's drawers while they were at work.

Sometimes we'd even go to a movie. We both love black-and-white films and marvel over the chiaroscuro lighting of the cinematic classics. Whenever Alfred Hitchcock is playing at the Rialto, we're there. Whoever's the first one to spot him in his famous cameos gets to pick an accent the other person is forced to use for the rest of the day.

One day, after *Suspicion*, we sat in the theater and stared at the empty screen. Finally, Maddie spoke, using a Spanish lilt. "*Mee-lee*, I know you're not sick. So why don't you tell me why you don't want to go to school?"

"But I am sick." I tried to look pitiful. Actually, I was feeling ill, having washed down a box of Goobers and a medium-size buttered popcorn with a jumbo Cherry Coke.

Maddie put her hand to my forehead. "Bambino, you're not sick," she said. We sat there for a while longer and watched the usher going up and down the rows dragging a trash bag behind him. He wasn't happy. "Is it the homework? Is it too hard?" she asked.

I started to giggle. "Right. Like multiplying three-digit numbers is soooooo difficult."

The usher looked at us and shrugged. We were the only ones left in the theater. "If you want to see the movie a second time, you have to pay again," he said. "Or you could just give me two bucks and I won't report you."

Maddie rose stiffly. "We're on our way out."

For someone who prides herself on her arrest record, she has a strange code of ethics.

"Is it your teacher?" she asked as we exited the theater. I was momentarily blinded by the sunlight. I opened my eyes and squinted. From where I stood Maddie looked silhouetted, like she had a mystical aura around her. "Hmmm . . . So, it's the students then," the all-knowing Buddha said. "You know, Millicent, they can't hurt you if you don't let them. Though it's hard for you now, facing your tormentors will build your character. If you run from them, they will chase you. If you face them, chances are they will be the ones to back away."

I didn't answer, instead pretending to be fascinated with the "Coming Soon" movie poster for *The Man Who Knew Too Much*. Perhaps it should have read *The Maddie Who Knew Too Much*, for she was right. If I wanted Digger out of my life, I'd have to stop running away from him and do something about it. That night, I began planning my salt-shaker revenge.

My poetry class is something I will never flee from. Today we studied Matsuo Basho, the famous haiku master. Even with his economy of words, his works are immensely exquisite and insightful. When Professor Skylanski read aloud some of his haiku I found myself so deeply moved I almost forgot to take notes.

For extra credit I composed my own haiku. Professor Skylanski was so taken with it she read it to the class.

Plague upon my life
Oh, stupid, stupid Stanford
Empty-headed boy

I think Emily is starting to suspect that all is not what it seems. She asked me what I do with my mornings when we are not together, so I hurriedly ad-libbed some ambiguous things about summer school and nouns and verbs, and then pretended to be absorbed in untangling the knot in my shoelace.

"What summer school class are you taking?" Emily asked as she waved good-bye to Julie. We had just finished volleyball and didn't do half bad. Even Coach Gowin said so. "Why are you going to summer school if your dad homeschools you?"

"I'm just taking an English class," I mumbled. "English isn't my dad's best subject." Which is the truth. He always gets Thomas Wolfe and Tom Wolfe mixed up, even though their writing styles are entirely different.

"You should talk to Alice then," Emily suggested. "She's read just about every book ever written. She knows everything. It's such a pain. Do you know what it's like living with someone who knows everything?"

I had a pretty good idea.

The strangest phenomenon has occurred. I almost enjoy volleyball. To my amazement, Coach Gowin's advice actually works. When I run up to the ball instead of away from it, my game improves immensely. And while I haven't mastered spiking, I've discovered that I am not half bad as a setter and that nearly one-third of my serves now make it over the net. Nothing thrilled me more than this afternoon when my teammates shouted, "Great serve!"

Meanwhile, my father and Emily have got some sort of *Three Stooges* thing going, except it's only the two of them. Whenever they see each other they start goofing around, making peculiar whippoorwill-type noises and pretending to poke each other in the eyes. Though I fail to find the humor in potential corneal abrasions, they seem to think this is hilarious.

Dad and Emily are also skateboard, Frisbee, and Nerf Ball fanatics. Yesterday my father was trying to teach Emily an under-the-leg Frisbee catch as I watched from the sidelines. "Come on, Millie," he called out. "I'll teach you how to throw a Frisbee."

I pretended not to hear him. Though I admire the aerodynamics of the Frisbee, which began as an ordinary pie tin, I was not intrigued enough to actually want to fling one in the air.

"Yes, come play with us," Emily insisted as she caught a high-flying throw.

The two of them looked like they were having so much fun. I didn't want to interrupt, so instead I feigned interest in the beaded bracelet I was making as a bon voyage present for Maddie.

Whenever Dad and Emily try to include me in their reindeer games, I decline. However, if they beg, it's possible I might give in just to appease them. But they don't ask much anymore, so I don't bring it up. It's no big deal, really. I just wait in my tree and watch through my binoculars until they are done with their childish hijinks.

Today, while my father was trying to rig a clock to run backward, Emily called with some big secret. She said it was something she couldn't even begin to discuss over the phone. I wondered if maybe her dad was coming back. She really misses him but is afraid that if she tells her mother, Alice will feel hurt. So instead Emily doesn't talk to her mom at all.

We met at the food court in the mall. For the longest time Emily just sat there poking at her Cinnabon. It was really starting to bug me because I strongly believe that if one orders dessert, one should eat it. Finally, she dragged her chair right next to mine and whispered, "I started my period."

I didn't know what to say. Was I supposed to congratulate her or tell her I was sorry? I don't suppose there's a Hallmark card for this sort of thing. I mean, what would it read? "A standing ovation for your first ovulation!"

Looks are deceiving. Emily is twelve, but she looks like she's fourteen. I am eleven, but I look like I'm nine. Maddie keeps trying to convince me that it's a blessing to look younger than you really are. "You'll appreciate it when you're a woman," she says. Like that day will ever come.

Emily wears a training bra. What she's in training for, I hesitate to even think about. I am convinced I will never grow breasts. I am a stick. Even tights are loose on me. Mom says it's good to be flat, that way you can go running and not have to worry about your breasts bobbing up and down. So now I have to take up running to appreciate my flat-chestedness. Actually, I can't wait to grow up. Maybe when my body catches up to my intellect, life will be easier.

"It's all so unreal," Emily wailed, giving me a poke in the ribs to make sure I was paying attention.

"What did Alice say when you told her?" I asked to be polite. Even though I found the topic a bit unsettling, Emily seemed fascinated by it.

Emily rolled her eyes upward. "She cried," she said as she picked at the frosting of her Cinnabon. "She actually cried and said, 'You're not a baby anymore.'"

I gave this some thought. My mother had said that same thing when I was two and mastered double-digit multiplication.

"Do you feel different?"

Emily wrinkled her nose. "I feel totally different, and the same. Plus I feel like I have a weird stomachache, you know," she looked around to make sure no one was listening, "*down there.*"

Oh God. The last thing I'd want is a stomachache down there. I've had enough problems with my ulcers. Luckily, they are now under control thanks to the Herbal Lew Lum Luck Stomach, Ulcer, and Gastritis Sedative that Maddie had her friend the herbalist prescribe for me.

Emily looked distracted as she nibbled on her Cinnabon. She kept shifting around in her chair and then whispered, "I'm wearing a maxi pad, but I don't want to talk about it." I was glad she didn't want to pursue the subject any further. It was making me uncomfortable. Then before I could change the subject she blurted out, "Alice says I'm not ready for tampons."

As Emily waited for a reply, it was my turn to squirm in my chair. What exactly did she expect me to say? "I really don't know anything about feminine hygiene products," I confessed. "But maybe you could talk to my mom."

Emily brightened. "Maybe I will," she said, taking a big bite of her Cinnabon. "She's so easy to talk to."

I tried hard to think of something highly personal to tell Emily, since she was being so candid with me. Nonetheless, I couldn't think of anything, other than that I was a genius. Yet somehow it didn't seem like the appropriate thing to say. So finally I came up with, "I thought I had a zit this morning, but my mom says it's just a bug bite."

Emily scrutinized my face and confirmed what my mother had said, adding, "If you put some toothpaste on it overnight, it will disappear, unlike the cramps and PMS, which go on forever. That's why they call it *the curse*. . . ."

I pretended to be paying attention as Emily droned on and on about her period. However, I was really thinking about what would happen to me if/when I started mine, which, at the rate I am growing, will probably take place in about fifty-three years. Of course my mother would expect me to tell her immediately, and Maddie will somehow know about it even before I do. As for Dad, well, it's exactly the sort of thing he wouldn't want to hear about. He is a master at avoiding what my mother refers to as "issues."

Yesterday Dad came home in a great mood. He's been invited back for a second interview. "That's terrific, Jack!" my mom said, giving him a kiss. Yech. I hate it when they do things like that in front of me.

"Good going, Mr. Min!" Emily said with so much enthusiasm you'd have thought he just won the lottery and offered her half.

"Congrats, Dad," I told him, shaking his hand. "Remember

not to take it too seriously. You never know how things will end up, even if you have the best intentions." I decided to take a break from the Famous Astronauts puzzle Emily and I were working on and give him a pep talk. "You know, Winston Churchill did not become prime minister of England until he was a senior citizen, and Albert Einstein failed his first college entrance exam. So don't worry if you don't do well on this next interview, I'll be proud of you no matter what!"

My father abruptly excused himself and went into his den to tinker with the computer he's been building. He's worked on it for months and uses it as an excuse for his endless trips to Radio Shack. Dad knows everyone there and they let him go behind the counter and into the stockroom, even though it's supposed to be for employees only.

"I think you hurt his feelings." Emily found part of John Glenn's chin and attached it to the rest of his face.

"No way," I told her. "I was trying to cheer him up. He likes it that I can be totally honest with him."

Emily completed the Sally Ride section. She is better at puzzles than I thought she would be. "Well, still," Emily said, not sounding totally convinced, "he seems a little worried."

Was he worried? Now that Emily brought it up, Dad did seem rather distracted when he left the room.

Not to brag, but I can see why Professor Skylanski likes me so much. I am a good student, I do all my homework, I prepare for class, I answer questions, and I ask for extra work. Unlike Stanford, the human driftwood.

So there I was drilling Stanford on plot when who should stroll into the library, but Emily.

"Ohmygosh, Millie, what are you doing here? I just came to get my library card. And . . ." she stopped herself when she saw Stanford and gasped. "Uh, oh, hello there! I'm Emily, Millie's best friend, I don't think we've met."

I glanced at Stanford, who looked as if an army of red ants had just been released into his pants. Before I could say anything, he startled me by leaping up and vigorously shaking Emily's hand. "Stanford Wong," he boomed. "I'm just, uh . . . uh . . . I'm just helping Millicent here with her studies."

What?!!!

"Excuse me!" I said as the two of them stood there like idiots grinning at each other. Their eyes remained locked and neither took the cue when I said repeatedly, "We really should be getting back to the books."

After a protracted silence in which Stanford and Emily continued to look stupid and remain speechless, he blathered, "Um, Emily, I'm sure Millicent would prefer it if you weren't here during our tutoring sessions." He blushed and lowered his voice. "She gets embarrassed." Emily looked crestfallen. "Of course," Stanford quickly added, "if Millicent ever figures out the difference between plot and theme, then maybe we could all get together afterward. You know, get a burger or something."

"Oh! That sounds like a terrific idea. We'd love to go," Emily said, speaking for the two of us. "We love hamburgers."

Great. One look at Meathead and my best friend has already transformed me from a vegetarian into a carnivore.

Emily glanced over at me. Sensing my distress, she took me aside. "It's okay, Millie," she said, draping her arm over my shoulder and giving me a quick squeeze. "Not everyone can be a genius. I don't think any less of you because Stanford has to tutor you. It's that English class you're taking in summer school, isn't it?" She took my stunned silence for agreement. "I'm sure it's a really hard class if your dad can't help you. But truly, there's nothing wrong with admitting that you're not the smartest person on the planet. In fact, I think you're very brave to ask for help. Now a lot of things make more sense. You know, why you're so secretive and always trying to use big words."

I could see Stanford frantically signaling me. He held up the contract I had signed, swearing on my mother's life that I would not tell anyone that I was tutoring him. "Thanks for understanding," I muttered to Emily as I made my way back to the table.

There was no point in even attempting to finish the tutoring session. Emily promised to "give us some space." To her this meant roaming around the library, giving me little waves. Knowing he had an audience, Stanford intoned, "Millicent, you should know this by now. Why is foreshadowing important?" Or, "Millie, Millie, Millie, haven't I taught you anything?" It was more than I could bear. So when I suggested we cut the session short, both Emily and Stanford immediately agreed it was a great idea.

At Burger King I just sat and seethed as Emily and Stanford talked nonstop. I have never known him to be so upbeat and friendly. He seemed almost human.

"Gosh, Millie," Emily whispered as Stanford went to get some more straws. They had been shooting straw wrappers at each other and confused this with having fun. "He's cute and smart and athletic, what more could you ask for?"

"Someone of our own species," I said under my breath as I poked at the ice cubes in my Coke. Regardless of how many

times I pushed them down with a coffee stirrer, they kept bobbing back up to the surface.

Stanford came back grinning. "Hey Emmie, lookit!" He held
up two fistfuls of straws.

Emmie? Oooh, he was really pushing me over the edge. I sat up
straight and informed him, "One: 'Lookit' is not a real word.
And two: It's stealing when you take things and don't use them
for their intended purpose. Plus, consider the unnecessary waste
and its impact on the environment."

Emily bit her lip. "I guess we really shouldn't waste them."
She looked disappointed as she set down her straws.

"Fine. Great. Terrific. I'll just put them back then," Stanford
huffed.

"Hey," I said sweetly, "I am only trying to help save our
planet."

When Stanford returned he was wearing a Burger King
crown, only he still looked like a jester. He handed us each one.
Emily put hers on immediately. I tossed mine aside.

"Emily, watch this," Stanford said. He opened up the napkin
and pressed it against his face. Then, and this was so gross, he
stuck his tongue through it.

Emily burst into a fit of laughter. Then she tried the disgusting napkin spectacle and Stanford started laughing like a hyena,
only not as dignified. "Here, Millie," Emily said, handing me a
napkin. "Your turn."

They both looked at me expectantly. I held the napkin to my face and then daintily wiped my mouth. "If you two will excuse me," I said as I pushed my chair back and stood up. "I think I hear my mother calling."

I grabbed my briefcase and stormed down the block. Emily was out of breath by the time she caught up with me. She looked concerned.

"What's the matter? Did I do something wrong?" When I didn't answer, her face clouded over. Then all at once she lit up. "Oh, I know. I just figured it out."

I waited to hear what she would say, hoping that she had realized what a dolt Stanford was.

"You're still feeling bad because I found out that he's tutoring you. It's okay, really it is," she assured me. "Millie, we're best friends, remember." She touched her friendship necklace. "Nothing can come between us, okay?"

Nothing but Stanford. That dumb boy could ruin my entire relationship with Emily. Not that he'd want her to know that he was the one being tutored. Still, he couldn't be trusted. By the way they were acting at Burger King you would have thought that they were the old friends and I was a stranger who just happened to be sitting at their table having a miserable time. I was reminded of my last party, a festive occasion for all but the birthday girl.

I've asked my parents to stop giving me birthday parties

because no one ever shows up and then we are forced to use the napkins that read "It's Your Big Day, Birthday Girl!" for the rest of the week. At my eleventh birthday party, my parents somehow managed to trick some kids into coming. My father dressed as some sort of cowboy-spaceman, I couldn't tell which. I think my mom was upset by this because the theme was *Gilligan's Island.* She's excellent at theming. People still talk about my parents' wedding. The theme was *Strawberry Fields Forever,* so you can just imagine what that must have been like.

For my party, Mom had planned lots of games with fabulous prizes. I won only one, Catch the Castaway, by default. I hid so well that everyone quit looking for me and the party went on without the birthday girl. Finally, when I emerged from my hiding place (in the closet, behind the steamer trunk, under the blanket), the only person left was Max, the annoying little neighbor kid. He admires me because he thinks I live in a tree.

I was told that my guests had a good time. My mom saved a coconut for me. I still have it, but it dried up inside and is beginning to stink.

"MILLICENT!"

"Huh?"

Emily looked worried. "I'm not sure where you go sometimes," she said. "You just space out."

"Well, I'm here now!" I assured her. I was glad she had left

Stanford. Maybe we'd go to my house and break in a new jumbo bag of chips. Or we could go to the park and hang upside down on the monkey bars and see who can last the longest. I've won three times in a row.

"Come on back and join us," Emily said, picking up my briefcase. "Stanford claims he can put a whole Whopper in his mouth at once!"

I couldn't believe she wanted to go back to that dimwit. "No, you go ahead," I insisted as I took my briefcase from her hands. "I have a lot of stuff I need to do."

"Are you sure?" Emily asked.

"Yeah, go on without me," I said, hoping she would stay.

"Well, okay then . . ." Emily said. "You sure you won't join us?"

"Positive," I said. *Please stay, please stay.* "I've got a lot of things to do."

"All right then, see you tomorrow, I guess." Emily looked confused. She held her crown so it wouldn't fall off her head as she hurried back to Burger King.

Why, I wondered, was it so hard just to tell her what I was thinking?

With no place pressing to go, I headed to the park. It was empty, except for a boy clinging to a tire swing as his friend spun him so quickly he looked like triplets. When he finally got off, he wobbled and then fell down. His friend helped him up and then they slugged each other and ran off. Friendships are so confusing.

I set my briefcase down and approached the monkey bars. Then I hung upside down until I couldn't tell what was upright, me or the rest of the world. I broke my own record by three minutes, only there was no one there to confirm it.

It's happening faster than I had anticipated. Maddie announced her plans less than a month ago, and already it seems like she's practically halfway to Heathrow, the quaint English hamlet that's now the site of one of the world's busiest airports. From there, it's a short hop to Fenwick & Feldie's Feng Shui Academy in the heart of London.

Maddie was humming as we cleared out her closets today. She hums when she is happy and it had been a while since I had heard her hum. I picked up the gilded frame that held Grandpa's mug shot and studied it. In the photos my grandfather is grinning mischievously. Though it vexes my mother to see it, I think it's one of the best pictures of him ever taken. I like to look at it since it shows his face, front and profile.

My grandmother is going to put her things in U-Pak-It—We-Stor-It. When she returns she plans to move into a smaller place — "like your den," she joked to Dad the other day. He almost spit out his root beer.

"It's just not the same here anymore." I could see that Maddie was trying to explain it to herself as much as to me. "There's no laughter to bounce off the walls."

I am going to miss that house. It is my second home. How can I ever forget the kitchen where Maddie taught me how to make microwave brownies? And there's the telescope that Grandpa and I gazed through on clear nights. He'd always ask, "What do you see up there, Millicent?" And I'd answer, "Everything, Grandpa. I see everything."

"When will you be back?" I asked Maddie as I examined an old photo of my parents waving at a marching band while I sat on the curb reading a book.

"When the time is right." She tried to look mysterious by arching her eyebrows. Whenever my grandmother does that it means she doesn't have the answer.

Maddie has agreed to stay in Rancho Rosetta until the end of the summer. Then, once school starts, she will be on her way. It was her idea to start packing now, "a little each day." She was sitting in an empty box when she said this, and I wondered if she planned to have herself shipped to England. Nothing she does could surprise me.

Maddie exited the box and then struggled to open the lid of her Chinese camphor chest. I had never seen the chest open before. The lid creaked and inside it smelled sticky-sweet. "Let's see what we've got here," she said, rubbing her hands together.

"You know, Millicent," she pulled out a pile of yellowing newspaper clippings and gently placed them on the floor. "Emily paid me a visit this morning."

"Why?" My curiosity was piqued. Emily and I often visit Maddie, but she had never gone by herself before.

"She wanted my advice," Maddie said nonchalantly.

"About what?"

"About you.

"When Emily told me she knew all about your big secret, I was so pleased that you had finally found the courage to tell her. Emily is such a kindhearted girl. She kept saying that it didn't matter how smart you were, that she was your best friend and that she wanted to make sure you weren't feeling bad that she had found out.

"But then when she asked, 'How long has Stanford been tutoring Millie?' I was speechless. Can you imagine? Me speechless?"

I admitted that I could not.

Maddie stopped digging in the chest and looked straight at me. "She doesn't know, does she?"

I didn't know what to say. I hadn't planned on Emily stumbling into my tutoring session with Stanford. "I was going to tell her," I insisted. "But then Stanford made me swear not to. . . ."

Maddie turned away. "Millie," she said softly. "Emily is a friend worth keeping. I trust you will do the right thing."

"I'm not too happy about this either," I said glumly. To have Emily think that Stanford is teaching me is beyond insulting.

We continued to pack in silence. I prayed that Maddie would say something, anything, but she didn't. Sometimes she talks so much, I can't stand it. But it's even worse when she doesn't talk at all.

Finally, Maddie reached the bottom of the chest and pulled out a beat-up old stuffed animal. "Look, it's Chow Lee Low!" she said, holding up the dusty yellow dog for me to see. "He used to be your mother's. She kept him around until she went off to college and met your father. I guess Jack replaced him."

I looked at Dad's competition, all ragged in his moth-eaten sweater. Like my father, Chow Lee Low had a charming but crooked smile. However, the similarities ended there, since Chow Lee Low's ears were droopy and he had one eye missing.

It was hard to believe that my mother ever had a stuffed animal. She has aged better than Chow Lee Low. "Your mom slept with him every night," Maddie said as she polished his remaining eye with her shirt. "He was her good-luck charm."

I almost started to cry. I will be so sad when Maddie embarks on her grand adventure. She is my good-luck charm, even if Dad's convinced she's just a crazy old woman. Just last week she tried channeling. That's where you "go back in time" to see who you used to be. The incredible thing was, Maddie claims to have come back as herself. What are the odds of that happening?

Mom says she's a force of nature and what Dad says about her I'm not supposed to repeat. What will I do without Maddie?

I think something is wrong with Mom. Okay. I've said it.

I've had my suspicions for some time now. There have been clues. Like last night I caught her just sitting on the couch. My dad does that too, but when Mom does it, it scares me. Usually, she's so full of energy she can never sit still. Even when she's relaxing she's always wiggling her foot or something. Then this morning I heard the unmistakable sound of someone barfing in the bathroom. When Mom opened the door, she looked flustered to find me standing there with my stethoscope.

"Oh hello, Millie," she said, trying to sound upbeat. "How are you?"

That's what I wanted to ask her. Only, if I did, it might be bad luck. You know, to bring it out in the open. Maddie says that if you don't want to know the answer, then don't ask the question. She was referring to how many grams of fat are in a box of See's chocolates, but I think her advice holds true in this situation.

I've often reflected on my relationship with my mother. Though she doesn't understand me and is quite accomplished at getting on my nerves, we share a strong mother–daughter bond. However, I've observed that sometimes she has a hard time deciding whether to act as a peer or a parent. This is a common occurrence among working mothers, so I try to be sensitive to her needs. Therefore, I refrain from bringing up subjects like death and estate planning.

On the few occasions when I have asked what would become of me if I were suddenly orphaned, my father has accused me of being morbid and my mother gets tight-lipped and says that in case of catastrophic illness or death I will be amply provided for. Still, I cannot stop my brain from thinking about what would happen to me if, say, my parents' airbags failed to deploy, or they accidentally ate some poisonous mushrooms, or if my mother has a fatal illness.

Maddie and I saw *Dark Victory* at one of our ditch sessions from school. In it, Bette Davis is this fun-loving society girl who discovers that she has a brain tumor. Her doctor falls hopelessly in love with her and we see Bette Davis change from a shallow, self-centered individual to someone full of love and depth. Then she goes blind and dies.

This morning at breakfast Dad was trying to scrape the last bit of apricot jam from the jar, and Mom was studying an ad for the Macy's Summer Sale. "I can't read the fine print in this newspaper," she said, squinting and moving the paper right up to her nose.

Immediately, I flashed back to blind Bette Davis and began to gag on my Pop-Tart. When my universal signal for choking — arms crossed, hands to throat — was ignored, I was forced to administer the Heimlich maneuver on myself. Luckily, I have my Red Cross first aid certificate.

All the while, my parents would not stop laughing. They thought I was joking. "Really, Millie," my father said, wiping his eyes with his napkin. "You are so dramatic. You must get that from your mother's side."

At that, Mom pretended to choke on her Cream of Wheat and they both burst out laughing again. I could have died, and they were laughing.

Almost 56 million people die each year. And more than 2.4 million of them are from the United States. After we lost Grandpa, I'd lie awake at night and worry about who might be next.

"Millicent," my mother said during one of those nights. "There are some problems that not even you can solve." Her hand felt cool as it stroked my hair. Some of our best moments are right before bed when we just talk or enjoy the silence.

Dad starts his new job soon. He's really nervous about it, and whenever we ask him questions he just yammers and changes the subject. I hope they like him there. I can tell this means a lot to him.

The other day at tutoring, Emily "just happened" to drop by. She also "just happened" to be wearing a new sundress and "just happened" to have a suspiciously deep dark tan, except for spots on her back and near her left ear. When interrogated, she finally admitted that she had used Barbados in a Bottle, a fast-acting bronzer with shimmering flecks of light. She was totally fake. Like I also really believed she needed to check out a book on the Los Angeles Lakers.

Stanford looked thrilled to see her. He promptly sat up straight and began grilling me on the importance of irony, saying things like, "Come on, Millicent, we've gone over this a thousand times before."

Then yesterday, Stanford showed up uninvited to volleyball, claiming he was "in the neighborhood." He just sat in the bleachers gnawing on what looked like his shoe, though later I found out it was beef jerky. Both teams tried to show off for his benefit, and the girls kept gawking at him. You'd think they'd never seen a dolt before. The whole time Emily kept whispering to me, "I can't believe he came to see us!" Afterward, she said to Stanford, "Millie and I were just going to get some ice cream." To which Stan-jerk replied, "Really? So was I." He's as fake as Emily's tan. Maybe the two of them deserve each other.

So the three of us go get ice cream and Stanford pays for Emily's, but not mine. The entire time the two of them were blabbing away as if I were not there. But the really amazing thing is they don't really say anything of importance. I mean, Stanford acted as if everything Emily said about the latest fashions and her theory that man did not really land on the moon was fascinating. And Emily got all wide-eyed when Stanford re-created his winning moves from his latest basketball game. Spare me.

When we are alone all Emily talks about is Stanford. "He's so cute. And his eyes, those big brown eyes look like Bambi's . . ."

"His eyes only look big because his glasses magnify them," I told her. "He's nearsighted."

". . . and his smile, he has the sweetest smile," she continued. Nothing I said was sinking in.

The only upside of this whole mess is that Stanford appears to be improving in his studies. The extra half hour of reading before basketball certainly helps, and these days he actually pays attention to me when I try to teach him something. He has to, because Emily's always asking him how our tutoring sessions are going. She just loves listening to him prattle on and on about topics he hardly knows anything about.

"Well, the theme of *Holes* is about belonging, isn't it?" he told her the other day. I pretended to have a coughing spasm. "And, as I keep telling Millicent," he said, raising his voice to drown me out, "*Holes* has a story within a story."

I can tell she is impressed. Emily thinks that Stanford is smart. And, ironically, around her he is.

Today at the library, I glanced at Stanford's notebook. There appeared to be drawings of Emily all over it. At least I think it was Emily. It was either her or an alien wearing the flowered dress Emily always wears, thinking it makes her look more alluring.

It is abundantly clear that Emily and Stanford have a crush on each other. All Emily talks about is how cute Stanford is. How nice Stanford is. How smart Stanford is. How boring.

"Say, Millie," Stanford said, looking up from *Holes*, "do you think I should cut my hair? You know, maybe get a buzz cut?"

I could not believe he was asking me that now. We were supposed to be studying. And why would he ask me? He never asked my opinion about anything before. He was acting very odd. Nicer. When we met in front of the library yesterday he was carrying a volleyball in addition to his usual basketball. It's ridiculous the way he is never without his basketball.

"What's that for?" I asked as I shifted my briefcase to the

other hand. It was starting to get heavy. Mom says I should take out the almanac, yet you never know when you might need one.

"It's to play volleyball."

"I know that," I bristled. "But why do you have one?"

"Well, I noticed that you could use some help with your serve."

"There's nothing wrong with my serve," I lied. Despite my dramatic improvements, there is still a lot wrong with my serves, and my sets and my spikes. However, this does not affect my efficiency as the team's official scorekeeper and statistician.

"Watch," Stanford said as he demonstrated the way I serve. I laughed because he looked like such a spaz. He retrieved the ball from the library parking lot and tossed it to me. "Here," he said. "You have to strike off your palm and the ball will go in the direction your palm faces. Okay, that's good. Now hit it."

I hit the ball and it wimped out, going straight toward the ground.

Stanford frowned. "Hold it again, and watch your palm when you strike the ball. And this time also bend your wrist backward, that way it'll go up higher," he instructed.

I did what he told me and watched in amazement as the ball formed a perfect arc in the air. We tried it a few more times and were successful. I wanted to keep going, but Stanford stopped me. "We'd better get to the library now," he said, looking at his watch. "I've got a book report due soon."

That Stanford is doing well in English is astonishing to us both. He has actually almost finished *Holes* and is well on his way with *Number the Stars*.

I have always been a reader. Mrs. Martinez, many of my teachers and, of course, my innate curiosity have led me to wonderful books. Even as a youngster, I was drawn to literature, choosing Katherine Paterson over *The Dumb Bunnies* and Sid Fleischman instead of *Barney and Friends*. As for comics, they are a genre unto themselves, and like my grandfather before me, I only read the classics.

When I was at Emily's a couple nights ago, Alice was puttering around in a fetching dashiki. Her feet were bare and I could see a new silver toe ring on her left foot.

"What are you working on now?" I asked her. I had noticed a pile of books about Shakespeare on the dining room table. Oh, how I longed to linger over them.

"William Shakespeare and his effect on young readers," Alice said, looking up from her laptop. "I'm tracking a group of inner-city youngsters who were exposed to Shakespeare at an early age and seeing where they are today."

"It sounds fascinating," I told her. "I'd love to hear more about it."

"Well, when I'm further along with the article, how about we discuss it?"

"I would love to!" How cool to be able to read an Alice X. Ebers article before anyone else.

"Are you interested in Shakespeare, Millie?" asked Alice.

"Oh, he's the best!" Just as I was about to rhapsodize more about the great bard, I stopped myself, remembering who I was supposed to be. A middle-school girl getting tutored in English because she is failing. "Or so I've heard," I quickly added.

"Yes," Alice said dreamily. "Brilliant and still topical, even today."

"Millie!" Emily yelled from her room. "Come in here, I need you *now!!!*"

"I'd better go," I said to Alice. I was reluctant to leave and I think she liked talking to me too. She seems sort of lonely.

"Okay then," Alice said, returning to her laptop. "We'll continue this conversation later."

"What's it like to have a hippie for a mom?" I asked Emily.

"I don't have a hippie for a mom. Do you think I should wear lip gloss?" Emily put some on before I could answer. "Do you think Stanford likes lip gloss?"

"You do so have a hippie for a mom," I told Emily. "Listen to her music. Look at how she dresses."

"Oh, that," Emily said dismissively. She started dousing herself with White Lightning. She had just bought the perfume with her father's charge card and spent so much that the lady gave her a free gift with purchase: a large white tote bag, a travel compact, a set of mini lipsticks, and a tiny comb. Emily wiped off her lip gloss and tried on one of the lipsticks. "That's not my real mom," she said, making kissy faces in the mirror.

I began to choke. I have many allergies and perfume is one of them. "Explain that," I said, trying to wave the offending odor away.

"Alice started dressing funny after we moved here. She's just going through another one of her phases. You should have seen her when she was in her career woman phase. She wore suits and pantyhose all the time. It was freaky." Emily turned toward me and got serious. "Tell me the truth," she said. "Which smile looks better? This one?" She did a big grin. "Or this one?" She smiled with her mouth closed.

I chose the toothy grin. Emily has been obsessing over her teeth. The dentist said she needs braces because her front two teeth overlap slightly. I have never given much thought to orthodontia, though I am probably destined to get braces since it is just one more thing to push me firmly into the nerd category.

I was six when I lost my first tooth. I thrilled at the notion that my primary dentation had passed and I was on to the beginnings of my permanent set of teeth. My father, on the other hand, spent the better part of a day trying to convince me to slip my tooth under my pillow. Finally, just to quiet him, I gave in.

When I awoke, my tooth was gone and a shiny silver dollar was in its place.

As I approached the breakfast table, Dad was downright giddy. "Find anything special under your pillow?" he asked, trying to sound nonchalant. My mother suppressed a smile, then returned to beating the lumps out of the pancake batter.

"Dad," I replied, attempting to let him down gently, "I know it was you who took my central incisor. Now may I please have it back? I'd like to study it under my microscope."

I tried to return the money. Of course, he refused the silver dollar and unconvincingly denied any knowledge about what I was talking about. A heated debate resulted and in the end I was once more in possession of my tooth, which I still have to this day.

My father looked dejected throughout the remainder of his breakfast and even went so far as to turn down seconds of buttermilk pancakes. The tooth fairy never visited me again after that.

Yesterday, while working on our lateral passes at volleyball practice, Emily confided, "Millie, sometimes I wish I were you. You're so lucky, you get to spend all that time alone with Stanford. What's it like when it's just the two of you? He's so incredibly gifted. I'll bet you could just listen to him all day. . . ."

In an effort to stop myself from yelling out the truth, I threw myself in front of the ball and, to the amazement of all, did an incredible dig.

"Keep up the good work, Millicent," Coach Gowin yelled.

That night, as we consumed penne pesto pasta with assorted vegetables (peas, squash, zucchini, and carrots), I studied Emily's mother. She was wearing a tie-dyed top and cutoffs. Her shirt, I noticed, still had its tag on, and she had paid full price.

Alice passed the garlic bread and asked me, "How are you doing with your schoolwork?" She had gotten her ears pierced again, making it a total of five holes. When I first met her I could have sworn she wore clip-on earrings.

"Just great!" I said. "With each class I find myself gaining a greater critical and aesthetic understanding of poetry and its importance to our society."

"Gee, that's pretty impressive for a middle-school student," Alice said, giving me an inquisitive look. I averted my eyes to my plate. "I'd love to talk to you and your father some day about homeschooling," she said. "It's such a big trend, maybe I can do an article about it and you two can be in it."

Panic. Total panic. "My dad's shy," I said quickly.

"He is not," Emily jumped in.

"I find it interesting that you go to summer school to supplement your homeschooling." Alice insisted on pursuing the subject. "Is it odd being the sole student in one venue and then being in a classroom full of kids for another?"

"Uh, no," I said, wishing she would talk about something else, anything else. "I hear melons are in season! Mom says you can get really good ones at the farmers' market. I am especially fond of honeydew, but you can't beat a ripe cantaloupe!"

"Emily tells me that you are also being tutored," Alice said, pressing forward.

I could hear Emily groan in the background. "Mommmm . . ."

"That's all right," Alice said, cutting her off. "Having a tutor is nothing to be ashamed of, is it, Millicent?"

I shook my head and speared four pieces of penne pasta, one on each fork tine. But Alice would not drop the subject. "It's great that your father recognizes he needs assistance teaching English, and to have that boy, what is his name . . . ?"

"Stanford," Emily and I muttered at the same time.

"Yes, for Stanford to volunteer to tutor you is so thoughtful of him. He must be a very nice and smart young man."

"Oh! He's supersmart," Emily chirped. "He knows everything about books. If it weren't for him, Millie would probably fail her summer school class."

I wondered if retching all over the table would be considered rude.

After dinner, Alice called me into her room. There was a king-size bed with mosquito netting over it and candles all over the nightstands. None were lit, nor had their wicks ever been singed.

Alice pulled something out of a bag and handed it to me. She looked pleased with herself. I stared at the book. It was *Ramona the Pest.* "If it gets too hard, I'd be happy to help you with the big words," she said, looking at me expectantly.

I started to tell her that I was actually close to finishing the biography of famed educationalist Maria Montessori. I thought it would help with my tutoring of Stanford. Then I caught myself, remembering my pledge.

"Thank you for the book," I managed to sputter.

When I got home, my mother was lying on the couch using my dad for a pillow. They were watching *The Lone Ranger.* "Hi,

Millie. Did you have a nice time at Emily's?" she asked. Before I could reply, Mom noticed the book.

"Oh! I love Beverly Cleary," she gushed, struggling to sit up. "I remember reading *Ramona the Pest* when I was a kid. It made me wish I had a sister."

"Shhhh," Dad said, "Tonto's in trouble and Silver is the only one who can save him."

My father loves *The Lone Ranger* and forces me to watch the re-runs. During the commercials I have to listen to him describe the cowboy costume he used to wear when he was a boy. He always ends his monologue with "I wish I knew where it was." As if it would still fit him.

Dad is really into telling me stuff about when he was a kid — a classic case of arrested development. Mom's not all that much better. She's keen on pointing out things like "When I was your age we had to bake potatoes in the oven because we didn't have microwaves." Or "Before remotes we had to get off the couch to change the channel." I'm not sure if I'm supposed to feel sorry for her or be grateful that I don't have to scrub my socks on a washboard.

As for my own childhood, it pretty much disappeared when I was two years old. That's when my parents had me tested. I had to take the IQ test twice since the first results were thought to be a computer glitch. "This little girl's IQ is so high it's an anomaly," my parents were informed. "She is nothing near normal."

Once my "genius" came to light, I was recognized as a celebrity of sorts. I was on television that same year reciting all the United States presidents. "In what order would you like to hear them?" I asked Jay Leno. "Alphabetical or by year in office?"

After a while, my parents felt the spotlight was not really a good thing for me. "Too much glare," I overheard Mom telling Dad. So they curbed my appearances and instead focused on my education. At my insistence, toys were replaced by books, and my favorite poster was not one of Elmo but Einstein. When I was three, I'd read to my parents (a favorite book of mine being Will and Ariel Durant's *The Age of Reason Begins: A History of European Civilization in the Period of Shakespeare, Bacon, Montaigne, Rembrandt, Galileo, and Descartes: 1558–1648*) until they fell asleep. Then I'd keep on reading to myself until my eyes betrayed me and I joined them in slumber.

The other day, Professor Skylanski asked me if I felt I had missed out on anything since I've been in school most of my life. "Missed out?" I said, trying not to snicker. "No, not at all. I consider myself lucky to be in college. Besides, I'm totally well-rounded. I have a best friend my age, Emily, and even another sort-of friend, Stanford. He's a boy, but not a 'boyfriend,' if you know what I mean. Plus, I'm on a volleyball team and no one makes fun of me anymore," I added proudly.

"That's really great, Millicent," Professor Skylanski said as she erased her Top 10 All-Time Poets from the blackboard.

"You're such a wonderful student, and I'm glad you realize that there is more to life than school. In order to truly appreciate poetry, one has to have a wealth of experiences to draw from."

I nodded. "Everything's going great," I assured her. And it was, other than Maddie leaving, my mother dying, and the tangle of lies I had gotten myself into with Emily.

Emily confided today that she feels rotten about her parents' divorce. Her father is already dating some "gold digger" with a daughter our age. Recently, he took the two of them to see the Radio City Rockettes. ". . . and if he bought them hot fudge sundaes afterward, I'll just die!" she howled as she punched her pillow.

I started to tell Emily that she was better off without her dad, but when I noticed that she didn't feel the same way, I changed my tactics. He still means a lot to her, even if she claims otherwise.

What I really wanted to tell her was about me, the real me. The geek-genius me, the me who's worried about my mom and who doesn't want Maddie to leave. I decided to lead into my confession slowly.

"Well, there is one good thing about you coming to Rancho Rosetta," I ventured.

"And that would be . . . ?" she asked as she continually applied and reapplied her LipSmackers.

"Me!" I said. "We wouldn't be best friends if you never came here."

There, I got her to smile. It's pretty great to be able to make someone smile.

"I like that we can tell each other everything and not have to worry about what the other person thinks," said Emily. Good, she was going to make this easy for me. "Like that Stanford is tutoring you. You were honest enough to own up to it. I can't tell you how much I admire you for that.

"I feel like you're the only person I can be totally honest with. If I try to tell Alice how I feel about Dad, she gets all weirded-out and cries." Emily looked like she was on the verge of tears. "Millie, you're so honest it shames me."

My stomach did the somersault that my body was incapable of doing during volleyball.

"Are you okay?" Emily looked concerned. "Are you sick? Should I get Alice?"

"It's just that . . ." I tried to speak but couldn't. "It's just that, I'm really not . . ."

Emily held up her hand. "Hey, it's okay," she said. "Whatever you have to say can wait until you feel better, all right?"

"Okay," I said, gasping for breath. "Yeah, it can wait. It's not important."

"She can't find out you're tutoring me," Stanford wailed.

"Emily'll think I'm stupid." I bit my tongue. "Besides, you swore on your mother's life that you wouldn't tell, remember?"

"Well, what about me?" I asked. "If she finds out I am a genius then she'll know I've lied and think I'm a total geek."

"That's true," he said, nodding solemnly.

"We have to tell her," I insisted. "She deserves to know."

"I don't like all this pretending either," Stanford said, biting into a Big Mac. We were at McDonald's lamenting our mutual problem. "But Emily really likes me. She thinks I'm smart. No one's ever thought that I was smart before." I nodded and sipped my chocolate shake. "There's just something about her," he continued. "She's different, but in a good way. When I'm around Emily I feel important." I knew what he meant.

"You know," I warned him, "when school starts you'll be seeing Emily on campus and she's bound to find out." Stanford let out a massive groan and pounded the table with his fist. Just then, the toddler at the next table spit up. His mother grabbed him and scurried to the bathroom, leaving their fries scattered all over the table.

"That was disgusting," Stanford noted as he mixed mayonnaise, ketchup, and mustard together and then dipped his pickle into it.

In the end, Stanford and I agreed not to mention anything to Emily, not just yet anyway. He wanted to do the spit-in-the-hand promise, but I assured him that I was good for my word.

In a strange way our lie has bound us together. Yesterday when we were at the mall with Emily, Stanford and I were both constantly on guard, helping each other so that our secret would not be discovered. At first I was upset to have Stanford popping up all the time. But for some reason, he doesn't seem as annoying as he used to be.

Lately, our tutoring sessions are not as excruciating as they were at the beginning of summer. Maybe I've grown accustomed to the pain, or maybe Stanford has actually learned a few things. He is making steps, albeit small ones, and I know he has the ability to do well if he sets his mind to it. Anyone who can analyze the performance of every player in the NBA can certainly appreciate the significance of plot, characterization, and theme.

Stanford actually wrote a halfway decent essay on *Number the*

Stars. When I told him so, he got all choked up and I was scared he was going to cry. "Really," he said, "Wow. No one's ever told me I was a great writer."

"I didn't say you were a great writer. I said this is pretty good, considering."

Stanford smiled and then added almost shyly, "Thanks, Millie. That means a lot to me, especially coming from you."

"You're welcome, Stanford." I caught myself smiling back at him.

Mrs. Martinez's squeaky book cart brought us back to why we were at the library in the first place. "Well!" I said, bringing us out of an awkward moment. "Let's go over your word list. . . ."

"It's amazing," I told Maddie today as she opened a fresh bag of Mint Milanos. "Stanford seems more tolerable these days. I wonder what's come over him?"

"Maybe you're more tolerable," she said, biting into her cookie with her eyes closed. She always closes her eyes when she eats her favorite foods. Maddie says it makes the food taste even better. She once ate an entire meal at Tandoori House blindfolded, much to the delight of my grandfather and the chagrin of my parents.

I looked at my grandmother as she sat across from me, lost in her heavenly cookie bliss. The other night Emily and I watched a *Kung Fu* marathon on the Rerun Channel. I had never seen *Kung Fu* before and was shocked. It featured a peaceful (except when he was fighting) half-Chinese, half-American man who grew up in a Shaolin temple in China. While he was there, a blind priest befriended him by calling him "grasshopper" and giving him words of wisdom that he constantly flashed back to in moments of moral crisis.

The curious thing was, I could swear that much of Maddie's sage advice has come from that television show. For example, she often says, "No one has ever died from being misunderstood." Did she think she could just lift those sayings from *Kung Fu* all these years without my finding out?

"Maddie," I said as I nibbled on my Mint Milano.

She opened her eyes and looked straight at me. "Yes?"

"Can I ask you something?"

"I know what you're going to ask."

"What?" Maybe she was clairvoyant after all.

"You want to know if the cookie really tastes better with your eyes closed, or if I'm just making that up." She handed me another cookie and I took it. "That is what you wanted to know, isn't it?"

I hesitated, considering whether to confront her or not. Then I shut my eyes and bit into the cookie. "Yes, that was it," I said with my mouth full.

Maddie was right, it did taste better that way.

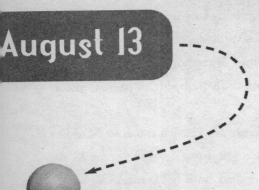

Who would have guessed that place mats would be my downfall?

This morning my mother asked me to get the good place mats out of the armoire. "Ummm, yes, I'll get to it," I mumbled. I was absorbed in trying to create anagrams with my Alpha-Bits, but the vowels kept sinking.

"Please have it done before dinner tonight," Mom added as she scooped up her purse, briefcase, and brown-bag lunch.

"Sure thing," I said.

Emily peered up from her cereal. Her letters were all jumbled and impossible to read. "I'll do it, Mrs. Min!" she said. Emily was continuing her mission to become the favorite Min daughter.

"Thanks, but no thanks, Emily. Millicent will do it. It's her job," Mom said as she downed her orange juice.

Dad poked his head into the kitchen. He was all dressed for work in his suit and tie. "Late again!" he yelled as he raced through, grabbing a piece of toast and the last banana. "See you girls later!"

Emily had spent the night. One of us is always at the other's house, though lately it seems like she's here all the time. I don't know what she finds so appealing about my cramped house. My parents are always acting up and forcing us to bake cookies or sing the "Pass the Old El Paso" jingle along with them.

At Emily's, Alice gives us our space, though I wouldn't mind spending more time with her. Sometimes, when she's not around, I sneak a peek at whatever she is working on. Naturally, I am careful not to ruffle through her papers, but rather, I merely glance at whatever is on top, or very near the top. Anything more than that would be intrusive.

"I'm going to get dressed," Emily announced. She was still in the monkey pajamas and matching monkey slippers her father had bought her, only he doesn't know it yet. I was wearing my cloud pajamas and had just managed to spell *smile* and then *slime.*

I pushed my Alpha-Bits around, making *miles* and *limes,* but Emily still had not returned. I hoped the washing machine hadn't overflowed. It happened once before and my room resembled the Johnstown, Pennsylvania, flood of 1889.

"Emily, everything okay?" I yelled. When she did not answer, I decided to see what the problem was. That's when I discovered Emily staring in disbelief at the dining room table. It was piled high with my trophies, certificates, and news clippings. She looked confused.

"What does this mean, Millicent? Are these all yours?"

I hesitated, not knowing what to say. But the proof was in front of her. I thought of the promise I had made to Stanford, and how I had sworn on my mother's life. "Tell me," she said, her voice rising.

"You were snooping!" I cried.

"I was not," she said. She stomped her foot, but because she was wearing monkey slippers there was no sound. "I was helping you out by getting the place mats out of the armoire and I pulled out these. . . ." She swept her arm over the booty like a game-show hostess.

Before I could tell Emily about the real Millicent L. Min, how I was a certified genius, how I was going to graduate from high school next year, how I was attending college for summer school, before I could even begin to explain my point of view, she became unhinged.

"Millicent, how could you do this to me?!!!" Emily yelled. "I heard rumors. Some kids at volleyball were talking. But I didn't believe them. We're never going to be in the same grade, you don't even go to middle school anymore. You're a genius, a stupid genius!"

I decided that pointing out her oxymoron would only serve to flame the situation.

"Millicent, when were you going to tell me? Are you even listening to me?" Emily shrieked.

It was hard for me to believe someone could bellow as long as she did. Unless, of course, that someone happened to be a banshee, the Gaelic folklore spirit who wails to warn of impending death.

I wondered if it was possible I had misjudged Emily's ability to comprehend my situation? After all, it was true I hadn't given her a chance. However, observing her histrionics made it clear that she would not have been able to handle it.

"Millicent!!!" Emily screeched. "What's the matter with you? Why are you just standing there? Well, aren't you going to say anything?"

What could I say? She was being totally irrational. As I paused to collect my thoughts, I noticed her face and neck turning a splotchy red. Still, I forged ahead. "Intelligence," I began, "merely refers to the all-around effectiveness of an individual's mental processes. . . ."

"Don't you get it?" she said, silently stomping her foot again. "Millicent, what is your problem?" I shrugged helplessly, not knowing what she was after. "It's not about how smart you are, it's that you didn't tell me! Didn't you think I'd find out? Didn't you think that it would hurt my feelings to be the last to know? Didn't you trust me? Didn't you think at all?"

When I hesitated, she took the opening as an opportunity to

continue her condemnation. "And why then, if you're supposed to be so smart, do you even need a tutor? Why does Stanford have to tutor you at all . . ." She squeezed her eyes shut and took several deep breaths.

I was about to offer her a calming mint or perhaps a jar of Mom's aromatherapy bath salts when she smacked herself in the forehead and shouted, "You lied about that, too, didn't you? Stanford's not tutoring you, you're tutoring him. Geez, Millicent, you're really something. I can't believe I thought you were my friend."

Emily grabbed her overnight bag and stormed out the front door, slamming it behind her. I was going to remind her that she was still in her pajamas, but I don't think she would have heard me.

Today I went solo for the first time in weeks. I refrained from telling Maddie and my parents about my falling out with Emily. The humiliation of them being right would be too much to bear. Also, with my mother's failing health, I do not wish to add to her burden.

I had nothing to do after poetry class, so I climbed up in my tree to work on some math puzzles. It was hard to get back into the rhythm and I tore up several pieces of paper in frustration, letting them fall to the ground. Max rode past in the station wagon just as another series of rejected cryptarithms drifted down from the tree. "Stop the car," he yelled to his mother. "It's snowing!!!"

Later I dropped by Maddie's. She always has plenty of snacks around and I was in desperate need of chocolate. There were boxes everywhere, and it looked like she hadn't done any packing since the last time I visited.

"Hey, how's it going?" I asked, gingerly sidestepping the Fiestaware.

"Slowly, but surely," Maddie said. She was sitting cross-legged on the floor going through an old photo album. "Every time I start to pack, I come across something that deserves my attention. Like this . . ."

I sat down beside her and we looked at her wedding photos in silence. She was so beautiful. Her hair was back in a bun and her wedding dress was simple and elegant. Grandpa stood tall beside her with a big sloppy smile on his face. He looked hand-some in his tuxedo with the white carnation. They both looked younger than my parents, which was a disconcerting thought.

"We had a small wedding," Maddie said, running her finger-tips lightly over Grandpa's likeness. "Just family and a few friends. Over the years, we collected friends the way other people collect stamps. We kept promising each other we'd renew our wedding vows and invite everyone we know. And this year I said to myself, 'This is the year we're going to do it!' But instead . . ." She left her thought in the air.

I recalled Grandpa's funeral. Once we said our last good-byes, six men, including my father, got up to carry Grandpa away. Maddie whispered that it was an honor to be a pallbearer and that she had a problem choosing since he had so many friends. I don't even have six friends.

I left her with her memories as I wandered through the house nibbling on a Baby Ruth. As I studied a picture my mother had drawn when she was a child, I detected some Impressionist influence. Or perhaps there was a bit of Picasso's Blue Period in Mom's vivid depiction of the whale — or was it a cow? Maddie came up and stood next to me. She smelled like gingerbread.

"I've always loved that picture your mother drew of me," she said.

I looked at it again.

After a while Maddie asked, "Have you seen Chow Lee Low?"

"Who?"

"Your mother's old stuffed dog."

"No," I said, wondering why she would think I knew where he might be.

Maddie frowned. "I must have misplaced him," she said.

My grandmother is always misplacing things. Once she misplaced Grandpa when they were on a car trip to Las Vegas. She drove off from a gas station thinking he was asleep in the backseat when really he was in the mini-mart buying Slim Jims.

"Where's Emily?" she asked, as if she too had been misplaced. "Say, aren't you supposed to be at volleyball?"

I held up my hand in a claw position. "Hand cramp," I explained. "Too many essays in my poetry class made it impossible for me to play volleyball today."

Maddie looked into my eyes, so I turned away in case she was going to try some of her psychic-cosmic mumbo jumbo on me. "Did you have a fight with Emily?"

"No," I fibbed. "Everything's fine, just fine."

"Okay then," Maddie said as she took her portrait off the wall and stacked it with the others. All that remained were rectangle imprints where the pictures used to be. "If that's what you say, then we'll leave it at that."

Any signs of Stanford being human have disappeared. *Poof!*

"How could you tell her?" He had gotten a buzz cut and reeked of cologne. Ode de Oaf, it smelled like. "Why did you do it? You swore on your mother's life!" he said accusingly. "What happened? Did you have a massive brain fart or something???!!!"

Mrs. Martinez looked up from her desk and signaled for us to keep our voices down, even though there was no one else in the library.

"I didn't tell her," I tried to explain as I gagged at his smell. I have very sensitive olfactory nerves. "I told you she found my certificates and diplomas. Hey, I just thought you'd want to know."

Stanford slumped back and glared at me as if I were responsible for his bad haircut. "Now I'll bet she hates us both. It's all your fault."

"No, it's your fault, I wanted to tell her the truth, but noooo, you wouldn't let me!"

The entire hour we ricocheted back and forth assigning blame and, needless to say, got in exactly zero minutes of tutoring time. I wondered if I could still charge his mother the seven dollars.

Just as we were about to come to blows, Emily walked in and headed straight toward us. Both Stanford and I shut up and corrected our posture. I started to stand to give Emily a hug, but saw the look on her face and immediately sat back down.

"Stanford. Millicent," she said, giving us each a formal nod. "I don't have much to say to either of you, other than I hope you had fun with your little charade."

Stanford opened his mouth, but Emily silenced him by merely raising her hand. I wish I had that power. She reached into her purse and pulled out *The Outsiders.* "Here, you can have your book back," she said, tossing it in front of Stanford. "Even though you raved about it, I don't think I want to read it anymore."

I looked at him in amazement. He had given Emily a book? A book that he had raved about? I started to say something, but then Emily turned to me. She reached around her neck and unclasped her necklace. The one that I had made at our very first sleepover.

"I think this belongs to you," she said, slapping it down on the table. I felt as though she had punched me in the stomach. "I hope the two of you have fun together making up lies. Good-bye."

Then she was gone. Stanford and I just looked at each other. I wondered if he felt as bad as I did. I wanted to talk to him about Emily and I wanted to talk to him about *The Outsiders*. But he didn't want to talk to me.

Finally, Stanford looked like he was about to speak. I waited for him to tell me that I was right and that we should have told Emily the truth before she found out on her own. Instead he said, "You're such an idiot," as he pushed everything off the table and stormed out of the library.

"You're such a cretin!" I yelled after him.

Mrs. Martinez looked over at me, but didn't say anything. I bent down and picked up the friendship necklace off the floor.

Imagine anyone even thinking that Stanford was my tutor. What a joke. As if there's anything he could ever teach me.

August 16

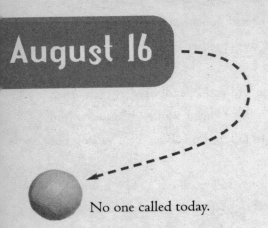

No one called today.

Nada.

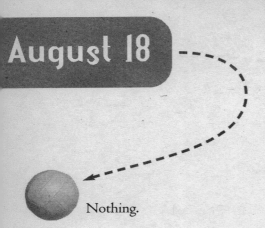

August 18

Nothing.

Not that I care, but it has now been 247 hours since Emily's dreadful hissy fit. I am determined not to call her, especially after the mean things she said to me. In the past I might have spoken to Maddie about this, but I can't tell her what has happened. I can't tell anyone, and the only ones who know are Emily and Stanford, and they aren't speaking to me either. I must remember to erase Emily from speed dial.

Volleyball has spun into a study in awkwardness. With Emily and I trying our best to ignore each other, our game suffers. One of us sets up the ball, and the other runs in the opposite direction. Coach Gowin is not amused. It is sheer torture being on the same court with Emily.

After volleyball the other day, Emily headed toward me. To my relief she was smiling. In return I sent her a huge grin. I was so glad she had finally come to her senses. But she brushed past me and joined Wendy, one of the nicer girls on our team.

"Ready?" Emily asked. She made a big point of not looking

at me. If she had lifted her nose any higher her whole body would have levitated.

"Let's go," Wendy answered, swinging her gym bag over her shoulder. "Millicent, are you coming too?"

My heart lifted as I rose to join them. However, my reprieve was cut short when Emily said in a snooty voice, "Millicent L. Min is too busy going to high school to want to spend time with dummies like us."

I felt a twinge in my chest. Wendy has always been friendly. Once Emily and I had even considered asking her to join us after a game. Nevertheless, to see the two of them walk away from me caused instantaneous peristaltic contractions that I diagnosed as pangs of hunger. Curiously, even after two U-NO bars and an open Yoo-Hoo I found in the refrigerator, I still felt unsettled. It's no wonder. There is just too much to think about.

I wish I could walk into Bob's Hardware Store and buy a shutoff valve for my brain. At bedtime my mind races. Thoughts pour out and dance around. Numbers add up and divide. Lists begin and never end. Songs without names taunt me. If my head could only be as empty as Stanford's, I would be able to slip into the delicious, deep sleep that eludes me.

The Idiot Stanford is bent on making my life even more miserable. He has stopped reading, instead choosing to sit and glare at me during our tutoring sessions. Therefore, I respond accordingly and glare back. The only person who is happy about this is

Mrs. Martinez, since Stanford and I are no longer yelling at each other. I can't believe I practically considered him a friend.

And life just keeps getting worse. I am convinced my mother is dying. Today I brought in the mail and saw the doctor bills, plus bills for lab tests. Her prognosis looks pretty grim. I've been compiling a list of her ailments. They are in line with the symptoms of a brain tumor.

MOM'S DIFFERENTIAL DIAGNOSIS — BRAIN TUMOR

Headache	Sometimes
Vomiting	Yes
Fatigue	Yes
Seizure	Not Yet
Blurred Vision	Yes
Mental Change	Yes

Mom tires easily, and Dad is acting all strange around her, as if she is fragile and going to break. I pretend not to notice.

My final for my poetry class is to write a thesis on a poet whose life reflects ours. I have selected Sylvia Plath, the talented, sensitive, intelligent but lonely and misunderstood young poet who committed suicide at the age of thirty.

After class today, Professor Skylanski and I had a long discussion about Ms. Plath. As we walked toward the parking lot, she must have sensed that I was contemplating more than figurative language. "Millicent?" she asked as she searched for her keys. From the outside I could see that her VW was littered with coffee cups. "Is there anything else on your mind?"

I chuckled and assured her that I had nothing on my mind. That my mind was a blank slate, an empty vessel, a dry well, devoid of conversational topics except for poetry. Though Professor Skylanski looked unconvinced, I urged her to leave so she would not be late for her lunch date.

As her vintage Volkswagen sputtered away, I waved and watched until it turned the corner. Then I tried to figure out what to do next. I could not go home right away. I was supposed to have volleyball, but I didn't feel like facing Emily. Plus, Maddie and my parents still think I have dinner at Emily's every Friday night. So I hung around campus instead. All day.

The place clears out pretty fast before the weekend. The few students who were left looked like they were getting ready to be someplace else. I wasn't hungry, so for lunch I sat in the cafeteria and nursed a chocolate pudding. I ate it with a fork to make it last longer.

At the library, the bank of computers sat empty as the Rogers College crest bounced around the screen. It was rare that no one was there, so I took advantage of the situation. I got online and researched famous females who grew up without mothers. The list includes the Brontë sisters, Marie Curie, and Madonna.

Afterward, I made a couple more laps around campus. I counted the buildings, and then the stairs. A small pebble lodged in my shoe, but I didn't bother to take it out even when it started to hurt.

As the afternoon wore on I spied Debbie and Craig goofing off on the grass, pushing each other, then hugging. Debbie spotted me. "Millie! Hi, Millie, come join us," she shouted as Craig tackled her and playfully covered her mouth.

I pretended I couldn't hear her.

All these years I've waited to go to college thinking that once I was there, everything would change. Everything would be better and I would finally find a place where I fit in. It is a cruel joke on me then that college is just like high school, only bigger.

It was starting to get dark and I had nowhere to go but home. I could see my parents through the window. They were getting ready for dinner. My father sat my mother down and then served her meal. When I saw him kiss her, I turned away to give them their privacy.

I watched the sun set from my tree, reading as long as the light would let me. As dusk began to fall, Max's father drove into his driveway and honked the horn. Max and his mother rushed outside. In the passenger seat of the sports car was a new yellow bike. Max hugged his father, and then hugged the bike, and then hugged his father again while his mother looked on, smiling.

My stomach made unattractive grumbling sounds. Luckily, I had my emergency Snickers bar in my briefcase. Even after eating it, my stomach felt empty.

Long after Max and his parents had gone inside, I climbed down my tree. My parents were eating popcorn in front of the blue glow of the television set. "What are you doing home?" Mom asked. She was in a giddy mood since Lucy was trying to say "Vitameatavegamin." *I Love Lucy* is Mom's favorite show, after *Jeopardy!*. "I thought you were staying at Emily's tonight."

"No, just for dinner," I said, rushing to my room. "I told you that."

"Did you?" she asked. As I shut the door I overheard Mom tell Dad, "I think I'm losing my memory now."

I won't even mention volleyball, except to say that Emily shouldn't have been standing there if she didn't want me to run into her.

Stanford and I have returned to our early days of tutoring where I try hard to teach him and he tries hard to deflect anything I say. Now that he's no longer out to impress Emily with his reading prowess, he's morphed back into a lump.

I made a chart to track the progress of our tutoring sessions. It resembled an EKG where the patient has died. Miraculously, the corpse spoke up. "I tried calling her, you know," Stanford muttered as he drew pictures of basketball hoops on his arm with a ballpoint pen.

"Here, use this," I said, handing him an indelible ink Sharpie. "What did she say?"

"Nothing. I couldn't go through with it. I hung up when she answered the phone. Emily seemed so angry the other day." He went back to drawing on his arm, this time adding little balls with the marker I gave him.

"I've been meaning to ask you," I said, "did you actually read *The Outsiders* before you gave it to Emily?"

Stanford stopped drawing long enough to glare at me. "Maybe I did and maybe I didn't," he answered. "That's for me to know and for you not to find out."

It's amazing how the days drag. If it weren't for the regularity of my summer school class, I don't know what would become of me. Professor Skylanski and I are developing a good friendship. Every day after class I walk her to her car and we talk poetry and literature and politics. I only have my college class three days a week. I wish it were more. I wish I had school twenty-four hours a day.

After today's class I went to visit Maddie. She was sitting in the kitchen with Julius, her wooden dragon. On the table were two plates of cookies and a pitcher of lemonade, as if she were expecting me.

"How did you know I was coming?" I asked, looking for a safe spot to park my briefcase. There were open boxes everywhere. The place looked like a giant rummage sale.

"I didn't," Maddie replied. She poured my lemonade into a tall frosty glass and handed it to me.

"Then why do you have two plates of cookies? You weren't feeding them to the dragon, were you?" I joked.

"Don't be silly," she said. "One plate for me, one for Grandpa." Maddie filled up her glass, took a sip, and then added four more spoonfuls of sugar.

I wondered if she was getting senile. That would explain a lot of things. "Grandpa's gone," I said gently.

"Then it's a good thing you came by to eat the cookies," Maddie said, giving me a wink. "Are you here to tell me the truth about Emily?"

"You know that we're not speaking?"

"I know that something's wrong," she said.

"Just tell me, tell me what to do," I groaned. I bit into a Lorna Doone shortbread cookie. There's something comforting about Lorna Doones. They seem so substantial, like they won't ever disappoint you.

Maddie took a slow sip of lemonade. "I can't. Soon I will be feng shui-ing Buckingham Palace, and you will have to make decisions on your own."

It was the first time ever that my grandmother hasn't weighed in with her opinion on a subject. I looked at Maddie to make sure she was okay. She seemed fine. The pendant with Grandpa's ashes was around her neck. She touched it from time to time and it seemed to comfort her.

"You have the power to make things right. But you must also be the one to decide what to do," she said, sounding very *Kung Fu*-ish.

I wondered if I had the power to make my mother better. I hesitated, wanting to ask Maddie about Mom, not even sure if she knew.

"How are things with you, Maddie?"

"Oh! Everything is fine. I got my passport today. Here, look. Don't I look pretty?" It was a nice photo. She looked happy. I never look good in photos, I always look so serious. The best pictures of me ever taken are the ones with Emily in the photo booth.

"And is everything fine with everyone else?" I asked, hoping that would open up a candid conversation about my mother and her demise.

"What do you mean?"

"Never mind," I said, reaching for another Lorna Doone. If Maddie knew about Mom, she probably wouldn't be planning a trip to Europe. Knowing her, she'd be moving in with us.

"Maddie really needs to go on this trip," I overheard Mom telling Dad. "It will be good for her. You know, give her some closure."

"Shouldn't we tell her?" he asked. "She'd want to know."

"No, not just yet," my mother said. "Besides, the doctor said not to say anything to anyone, just in case something changes. It's better that she doesn't know right now. I wouldn't want her to cancel her trip on my account."

For the first time in my life, I wish I didn't know so much.

This afternoon I found myself in front of the Rialto. *It's a Wonderful Life* was playing. That's what's so great about the Rialto. They play Christmas movies in the middle of summer, murder mysteries on Valentine's Day, and every Halloween there's a special midnight showing of *High Noon*.

"It makes no sense," I recalled telling Maddie as we watched Charlton Heston race around in a chariot last Labor Day. "That's why it makes perfect sense," she said before shushing me.

It's a Wonderful Life had already started by the time I sat down with my bucket of popcorn. It's a good movie. I'd seen it before. My favorite part is when Clarence gets his wings.

As the film ended I read the credits. Maddie and I always read the credits. "These people have worked so hard to entertain us, it's the least we can do," she says. When the lights came up and I rose to leave, I saw my father sitting alone in the back row.

"Millie," he said haltingly. "You're supposed to be with Emily."

"You're supposed to be at work," I said.

We walked out together and circled the block before either of us spoke.

"I didn't get the job," Dad confessed. I stopped mid-step and looked at him. A poster of Jimmy Stewart loomed large over his shoulder. "I just said I got the job so you and your mom wouldn't think I was a total loser." He looked so sad.

"You're not a loser," I protested. "But I don't get it. You mean you've been pretending to go to work all this time?"

"Pretty silly, huh? It's just that I don't want your mom to worry too much. Not now with . . ." His voice trailed off as I held my breath. "Hey . . . what happened to Emily?" he asked, abruptly changing the subject.

"Emily who?" I tried to joke. I continued walking so I wouldn't have to look at him. For all his goofiness, my father can be kind of intense sometimes. "Emily's not speaking to me," I finally confessed. "She found out that I'm a genius and is mad at me."

"She's mad because you're a genius or because you didn't tell her you were a genius?" he asked. Dad was starting to sound like my mother or, even worse, Maddie. When the three of them start sounding the same, I know I am in big trouble.

"She says it's because I didn't tell her."

"When did she find out?" When I told him it was the last time she slept over at our house, he barked, "Millie, that was almost two weeks ago! You've carried this around with you all this time? Why didn't you tell us?"

"I was afraid," I said. I felt small, like when I was three and broke Dad's compass while plotting a new path across the North Pole. Afraid to tell him what happened, I hid the compass in the freezer where it went undiscovered until Mom defrosted the refrigerator several months later. "I didn't know what you'd say," I blubbered. "I thought you'd say 'I told you so' or think I was just a big disappointment."

My dad stopped walking and faced me. I tried to turn away, but he wouldn't let me. "Millie," he said, sounding parental. "We love you no matter what and we'd never, ever think you were a disappointment. If you can't talk to your family, who can you talk to?"

I met his gaze. He looked so sincere. "You're right, Dad," I said. "If *you* can't talk to your family, who can you talk to?"

"Point well taken," he said. "Come on, let's head home. I think we both have some explaining to do to your mother." He hesitated, then added, "And Millie, one more thing." I waited. "You talk to Mom first, okay?"

"Sure, Dad," I promised as I hooked my arm though his.

Even though it was the middle of a weekday afternoon, my mother was in the kitchen sitting on the floor eating Rocky Road ice cream straight out of the container. She was supposed to be at work and obviously wasn't expecting Dad and me to be home either. When Dad cleared his throat, she let out a little yelp. Trying to hide the ice cream behind her back, Mom explained, "I wasn't feeling well, so I left work early today. Why are you two here . . . ?"

Mom was not the least bit surprised when I told her that Emily knew the truth and had dumped me. In fact, she said she wondered why it had taken so long for me to fess up. It is hard to fool that woman. She possesses mom-dar, which is an extremely powerful version of radar that the United States government would be wise to employ.

My mother also took Dad's news rather well, considering that he lied to her every morning when he left and then lied again at night when he returned. "So you haven't been going to the office all these weeks?" she asked, looking a bit mystified and more than a little annoyed. He started to say something but found himself without words.

Mom struggled to stand. "Whoa, I have to absorb this," she said, handing Dad the empty ice-cream container. "This one's a biggie." After a few moments of staring at the dirty dishes in the sink, she asked, "Why, Jack? Why would you go to all that trouble to make us think you had a job?"

I looked at the two of them and knew that the right thing to do would be to leave the room. It was clear that my parents wanted their privacy. However, I couldn't bear not knowing how it would end, so I pulled up a chair and opened a bag of Cheetos.

"Jack, I'd love to hear your explanation," Mom said. Her cool, even tone had a menacing effect.

Dad stumbled over his words as he tried to explain himself. Then he stood behind me and said, "Claire, I love you so much. I was embarrassed when I didn't get that big job. I meant to tell you, but as the days wore on it got harder and harder." I nodded vigorously, knowing what he meant.

As my father sputtered on, I watched my mother's face. A whole range of emotions flashed before me, starting with anger, then confusion, and finally ending with sadness.

"I'm your wife, your partner," she finally said. "If you thought I'd be upset with you for not getting that job, then you don't know me very well." Mom began to cry. "We promised to love, honor, and cherish each other in sickness and in health. . . ."

Dad stepped forward and hesitated before putting his arms around her. When she hugged him back, I could see his body relax. "I will never lie to you again," he whispered as he stroked her hair. "I am so sorry."

With my parents all lovey-dovey, I felt it best to get out of their way. It was inevitable that they would kiss at any moment and I didn't want a front-row seat. Still, I needed to talk. So I went to see the one person I had left.

Maddie was practicing yoga. She resembled a pretzel. "I am so glad to see you, Millie," she said. "If you hadn't come along, I might have been stuck here forever."

As I helped her unwind her legs, I told her what I was planning. "Very wise," Maddie noted, stretching her arms overhead.

"You have nothing to lose by apologizing and everything to lose if you don't." She attempted a scorpion pose, though it looked more like a series of donkey kicks.

As I bid her farewell, she called after me from her semi—upside-down position, "Millicent, before you apologize to Emily, make sure you know what you are apologizing for."

I nodded, pretending to know what she meant.

"And one more thing," she hastened to add. "Sometimes it's better to be liked, than it is to be right."

Even though I knew what needed to be done, it didn't mean I wasn't nervous. I waited a day so I could rehearse what I was going to say. I wanted everything to go "just so."

In order to ensure privacy, I took the phone into the hall closet. Calling from my room would be too risky. One never knew when the urge to do laundry would come over Mom. She was acting so strange.

I reprogrammed the speed dial and hit #4.

"Hello? Hello?" Emily answered. "Is anyone there?"

"Hi, it's me!" Though I felt tense, I tried to sound cheery.

"Me who?"

"Millie, silly."

There was a long silence and I wasn't sure if she was still there. At last, Emily asked, "What do you want, Millicent?" Her voice was ice-cold.

Since my cheery locution didn't have the effect on Emily that I had hoped for, I tried logic. "Well," I began. "I just thought that unless we both could afford the airfare to The Hague and the International Court of Justice, which of course is the principal judicial organ of the United Nations, our dispute —"

"Millicent, what are you blabbing about?"

This time the long silence came from my end of the telephone. Finally, I said softly, "I want to be friends again." (At this point I referred to the notes I had prepared, just in case.) "I'm sorry for whatever misunderstanding there was. I'm sorry you cannot comprehend my being a genius and a senior in high school . . ."

"You still don't get it, do you?" Emily said with a deep exaggerated sigh.

I could hear Alice in the background asking, "Who is it?"

"Nobody," Emily said dully.

"Is it the cable TV man?" her mom inquired.

"I said, it's *nobody*."

"If it's the cable TV man," Alice told her, "tell him that HBO doesn't work anymore but we still get Showtime."

I could tell our phone conversation was going nowhere, and I was anxious to make my peace with Emily. With Mom sick, Maddie leaving, my poetry class ending, Stanford turning back into a doofus, and Dad unemployed, I needed at least one thing in my life to go right.

"Emily, please," I begged, "can we at least meet and talk

about this? I promise not to take more than ten minutes of your time."

Emily and I rendezvoused near the food court at the mall. I had considered bringing a peace pipe, the truce symbol of the Native North Americans. However, since I did not have access to one and abhor smoking, I opted for a one-pound Jelly Belly assortment instead.

"No, thank you," Emily said, pushing my offering away. "I'm on a diet."

"But you're not fat, " I exclaimed. "And anyway, jelly beans are fat free."

"I am on a diet," she repeated firmly. I wondered if I could get my money back, or at least exchange it for chocolate.

"Well, I know that my being a genius can be off-putting," I began, dispensing with small talk. I had rehearsed my speech to last exactly ten minutes. "But I am certain our friendship is strong enough to withstand the effects of my high intelligence."

"Man," Emily interrupted, "for someone who's supposed to be so smart, you sure are dumb."

"Pardon me?" The reconciliation was not going as I had planned.

"Millicent, this is not about your brain." I tried to get her to lower her voice, but she was not cuing in on my subtle hand signals. "I'm mad at you because we were supposed to be best friends! But you didn't trust me enough to tell me the truth. Instead, you just assumed I wouldn't be able to handle it. There was this huge part of your life that you hid from me, even after I told you all about my fear of cats and that if I laugh too hard I wet my pants!"

"I can't believe you called me *dumb!*" I was stunned. "*Et tu, Brutè.*" (For dramatic effect I pulled an invisible knife from my back.)

"But Millie," Emily said gently, "you do act really dumb sometimes, like you're clueless."

I stopped to ponder the implications of her words. "So . . . ?" I challenged her.

"So nothing," she said. "It doesn't matter to me."

"Really?"

"I don't care if you're smart or dumb, as long as you're a true friend."

I fiddled with the Jelly Bellies. Admittedly, being called dumb did not sit well with me. "Emily," I finally concluded, "I'm sorry if I misrepresented myself in any manner. For you see, I had sorely misjudged the dynamics of our relationship . . ."

"Millie, you didn't just misjudge our relationship, you misjudged me," she cut me short. "Can't you just shut up and say you're sorry you lied without making up a bunch of hooey?"

I stopped my James Joycean stream-of-consciousness rhetoric. "Hooey," was that what she said? *Hooey?* Was she implying that I was making up nonsense, possibly as a screen to mask my true feelings? And "shut up"? How disrespectful.

I thought about how Emily never made fun of me at volleyball, or for not having other friends, or even when she thought I needed a tutor to get through middle school. It's possible she had a point. Perhaps I had misjudged her. In my frantic efforts to keep her as a friend, I was not a true friend to her. I hoped it was not too late.

"I am sorry I lied to you, Emily." I really was. There, I said it. Now it was up to her to decide if I was worthy of her friendship.

When Emily didn't react right away, I braced myself for a solitary life with cryptarithms to fill my days and only academic awards to befriend me. It had been so hard to say that I was sorry, and now that I had, a feeling of relief came over me. I felt as though I had just taken a test and there was nothing I could do but wait for the results. Only this time I was afraid I hadn't passed. I looked at Emily. She was all choked up. I turned to walk away.

"Hey!" she called after me, tugging on my shirt. "Where do you think you're going?" I stopped and turned around. She was right there with me. "I really missed you," Emily said. She gave me a big hug, and when I returned it twofold, we both pretended that we weren't crying.

"I always knew you were strange," she admitted, taking the

Jelly Bellies from me and fishing around for the black ones. "But I could never figure out why. Now I think I know . . ." I waited for her to tell me it was because I was a genius and that could be isolating. "It's because you're an only child, isn't it? Alice thinks that because I don't have brothers or sisters it has affected . . ." I just grinned as she went on and on.

It is so wonderful to have Emily back.

Last night Emily got the call she had been waiting for all summer. We were in her room alphabetizing her CDs (my idea) and had gotten up to *Mongo Bongo's Greatest Hits* when the phone began to ring. Though it was right next to Emily, she ignored it. My dad does that too and it drives my mom nuts. I was about to pick it up when Emily said offhandedly, "Oh, just let it ring. Alice will get it." I couldn't stand the incessant ringing, so I held my breath and was about to turn blue when all of a sudden . . . silence.

After a couple of minutes, Alice knocked on the door and opened it slowly. "Emily," she said. Her eyes were all red, like she had been crying. "There's a call for you. It's your father." Then she backed away and shut the door quietly.

Emily's face lit up as she dove for her phone. "Hi, Daddy!" she squealed. She kept pointing to the phone and mouthing, "My father." Emily's phone is translucent purple and you can see all the wires. My dad would love it. "Yes, uh-huh. Uh-huh,"

Emily turned to face the wall. "Okay. Sure! Yes! No problem! I love you too. Okay, good-bye!"

She kept her back to me for the longest time, and I couldn't tell whether she was happy or sad. That is, until she started bawling like a baby, making it pretty obvious.

Alice must have been standing right outside because in a nanosecond she was in the room hugging Emily. "It's not your fault, it's not your fault," Alice kept murmuring. I pretended I was mending a half–Be-Dazzled blouse I picked up off the floor.

"What did he say?" her mother asked. She brushed Emily's hair from her eyes. Emily just took big gulps of air and motioned for her to leave. I could tell that Alice was distraught, but she left us alone. She gave me a really sad look before she went away.

"Are you okay?" I asked. I wasn't sure if Emily knew I was still there, she was crying so hard.

Finally, she reached for the Be-Dazzled blouse and blew her nose on the sleeve. I was horrified, but calmed myself by rationalizing that it would wash out. "I thought he called to tell me he was coming back," Emily wailed. "That he wanted to say he had made a mistake. But nooooooo, Daddy just called because he wants me to stop using the credit card so much." She began to cry again.

I was at a loss over what to do, so I just sat there and handed her tissue after tissue until we had used up what was left of Emily's 150-count box of Puffs.

Realizing that my best friend needed cheering up fast, I resorted to desperate measures. "Say Em, why don't you do that makeover on me you've always wanted to do?"

Emily gasped and looked up through her tears. "Really?" she said, blinking wildly.

"Uh, sure," I said, hoping my voice would not betray my uncertainty.

I could not believe I had offered to let her do a makeover on me. But it was too late to back out. Emily was already up and gathering bottles and tubes and jars of makeup and whatnot.

"Sit here," she said, stifling her sniffles. "You are going to look so fabulous when I am done with you."

"Okay," I said obediently.

After what seemed like hours of being poked and plucked and painted, I stood in front of the mirror with my eyes shut.

"One, two, three!" Emily yelled.

I stared ahead, not knowing what to say. My hair was all poofed up on the top of my head, my lips were bright red and I had on green eye shadow. My cheeks were pink, and for some reason I had a purple rhinestone near my jawbone.

"Well . . . ?" Emily held her breath.

"Well," I began, still staring. "I look so different."

Emily let go a sigh and grinned. "I was so afraid you'd hate it," she confessed. "But I think it's the real you!"

"I'm not so sure about that," I told her. I was determined to be honest with Emily from here on out. "But it does show a side of me I've never seen before."

Just then Alice came by to see if Emily was all right. "I'm fine, Mom, *okay*?" Emily said.

"Just checking," Alice said quietly. I didn't think Emily needed to be so mean.

Alice looked me over and said, "Hmmm . . . interesting."

"Alice, *please*," Emily said, shaking her head.

"That's okay," I assured both of them. "Besides, it's not how you look that's important, it's how you feel. And I feel great."

"It's not how you look . . ." Alice murmured as she left.

Later I talked Emily into going to my house because she kept roaming around her room saying, "My father bought me that," and pointing to a lamp. Or "I charged that on my father's credit card," and pointing to a poster. It got to be pretty boring after a while, and eventually I got Emily to laugh by asking her to show me what her father didn't pay for.

As Emily packed her bag for a sleepover, I wandered into the living room. I didn't recognize the lady sitting on the couch at first. Alice was wearing a gray velour warm-up suit and Nikes. She tried to hide the Nacho Doritos and supermarket tabloid when she saw me gawking at her. "It's okay," I said. "I'm sure as a journalist you have to read everything."

Alice looked relieved. "That much is true, Millicent," she said, offering me some chips. I took a handful. Except for the crunching, we sat side by side in silence.

"I like your outfit," I finally said.

Alice scrutinized her clothes. "It's what I am most comfortable in," she said. "That carefree bohemian look is such hard work. Besides, as you said, 'It's not how you look, but how you feel.' And I feel most like myself in this."

I couldn't believe she was quoting me. We continued munching on the Doritos as we sat side by side, waiting for Emily.

After a powdery-cheese pause, I said, "So, I'm a genius."

"I know," she said matter-of-factly.

"Did Emily tell you?"

"Nope, figured it out on my own." Alice put down the Doritos. "You're quite an enigma, Millicent. A lot of things you said didn't add up. So I did a little sleuthing on the Internet. Remember, I write investigative pieces for a living."

"Why didn't you tell Emily?" I asked.

"It was clear to me you wanted to keep it a secret, so I decided to play along. Though it sure was fun giving you *Ramona the Pest*. You should have seen your face!"

"Actually," I admitted, "I really did like the book."

"I thought you would," Alice said, looking at her hands. The

Doritos had turned them orange. "Millie, please feel free to borrow any of my books you'd like."

"Really???!!!" I squeaked. I started making a mental list of the books I wanted to take first.

Just then Emily came out of her room dragging her big duffel bag. "You okay, Emily?" Alice asked.

"I'm fine, Mom," Emily said, eyeing Alice's outfit. She went over to her and kissed her cheek. "Are you okay?" It was the first time I had seen Emily show any concern for her mother.

"I will be," Alice said.

"Me too," said Emily.

My parents always look forward to the Labor Day Fiesta at the Wild Acres theme park. On that day, all Rancho Rosetta residents get in for half price. Mom and Dad claim the Fiesta gives them a good excuse to act silly. I'd like to know what their excuses are for the other 364 days of the year.

Maddie and Grandpa used to go to the Fiesta every year too. Grandpa declared that the Tunnel of Love was created in their honor. "The day we stop going," he proclaimed, "is the day they ought to shut it down." This year Maddie bowed out of going to the Fiesta. She said she had a headache.

I have never found the Fiesta to be enjoyable. Too crowded, too noisy, too juvenile. Still, when Dad and Emily begged me to go, who was I to let them down? I am attempting to embrace (or at least accept) change and have resolved to try one different thing per day. Yesterday I brushed my top molars first. Today, I accompanied my parents and best friend to a theme park.

Within minutes of arriving, my father parted with twenty-five dollars to "win" a small stuffed teddy bear for Mom at the B-Ball Bushel Throw. Do you know how many sheets of good graph paper twenty-five dollars can get you? Dad was proud of himself, though, and Mom was so thrilled that she didn't even flinch when I reminded her that you can buy a better-made bear for less than five dollars at the mall.

After wandering around the games and watching in horror as people lobbed Ping-Pong balls at innocent goldfish (does the ASPCA know about this?), we gravitated toward the aroma of deep-fried funnel cakes and roasted peanuts.

Mom immediately ordered a bratwurst with sauerkraut and peppers, even though we had just eaten lunch at home. My father opted for the homemade vanilla ice cream smothered with fresh strawberries. And Emily and I found ourselves in front of the cotton candy booth.

Every color of the rainbow was on display and I watched as the lady expertly twirled the pink sugar from the kettle onto a white paper cone. "They're four dollars each," she told Dad as he took out his wallet.

"Why, that's outrageous," I croaked. "Cotton candy is nothing more than spun sugar. I'll bet there's no more than one or two tablespoons of sugar on that entire cone. And how much does sugar cost? Not more than a few pennies!"

The cotton candy lady threw poison darts at me with her

eyes. Her aim was perfect. "You're holding up the line, missy," she said through a tight smile.

"Do you want one or not?" Dad asked, handing Emily what looked like a soft pink beehive on a stick.

"Okay," I conceded. I didn't want Emily to have to eat alone, though I resolved not to enjoy it too much since it was so expensive. Oh, but boy did it taste good. It was fun letting it dissolve on my tongue. Emily liked to tear off big chunks of hers, smash them up really small, like marbles, and then pop them into her mouth.

"You know," I said as we headed to the midway, "those games are rigged." I tried not to lick my fingers so that the cotton candy wouldn't get me all sticky. "Like the milk bottle throw. The bottles are weighted."

"Really?" Dad sounded genuinely surprised. He is so trusting. Mom just laughed and cradled her teddy bear as if it were a baby.

"I know they're rigged," Emily said, trying to get the cotton candy out of her hair and only succeeding in getting some stuck on her arm. "But it doesn't matter because they're fun."

Perhaps Emily had a point. The people playing the games did look like they were having a lot of fun. Despite every effort not to, I caught myself having fun too.

By the time we made our way to the rides, all that was left of the cotton candy was our sticky fingers and a pink glob the size of a yo-yo in Emily's hair. Luckily, I had the foresight to pack premoistened towelettes in my briefcase. But even that didn't help, so Mom had to pour water over Emily's head to get the cotton candy out.

As we neared the famed Monstroso Roller Coaster of Death, the four of us tilted our heads back and took it in as it zoomed around and around. The riders screamed like lunatics. It seemed so undignified.

"Wow!" Emily said reverently.

"I'll say," seconded Dad.

"Has it grown bigger since last year?" Mom asked. "I don't recall it being so big."

"C'mon, what are we waiting for?" Emily shouted, running to get in line.

I held back. "It's okay, Millie, you don't have to go if you don't want to," Dad whispered. I know we were thinking the same thing.

I get dizzy easily. When I was three my father put me on Binky, a carousel horse. I didn't want to go and screamed so loudly they had to stop the merry-go-round. My father rode Binky the rest of the way by himself.

Perhaps I have vertigo, like Jimmy Stewart in the movie of the same name. In it, his fear of heights causes him to get dizzy whenever he is up high and looks down. And if that's not annoying enough, he has the hardest time sorting out reality and illusion, sort of like Maddie when she eats too many Moon Pies.

Emily kept waving at me. "C'mon, Millie, hurry!"

I turned to my mother. She was studying the warning sign. "Aren't you going?" I asked. Mom usually loves roller coasters.

"No, honey," she said wistfully. "I think I'll sit this one out this time. But you go right ahead." She paused and then gave me a gentle nudge. "Go on."

I looked over at Dad who had joined Emily. He was staring up at the top of the roller coaster. His jaw was slack. Every year he has talked of conquering Monstroso by holding his hands up in the air during the entire ride, just to show it who's boss. He had yet to do it.

Emily was still waving frantically. "Hurry!" she shouted. She looked funny jumping up and down, like one of the targets at the shooting gallery.

To go or not to go. That was the question. Just then I saw some boys from Stanford's basketball team. They were looking my way, and the carrot-topped one started doing a pitiful imitation of a chicken.

What if Stanford were here, I wondered. What if he were watching? I'd never hear the end of this. The carrot-topped boy began to squawk louder. Something about him made me feel uneasy. "Coming!" I shouted to Emily. "Wait up!"

Though I knew that the centripetal force would weld us to

the seats, I was unprepared as the roller coaster made its first plunge into a loop-the-loop. As the cars free-fell and turned upside down in excess of fifty miles per hour, my stomach churned and my hands melded into the safety bar. My face hurt from the wind whipping my hair. I was glad I had just updated my last will and testament.

Turning toward Emily, I could see that she was scared out of her wits too. The wind had dried out her hair, and her face was frozen into the kind of look you hope no one ever captures on film. She glanced my way and then we did the only reasonable thing we could. We screamed for our lives.

With each death-defying plunge of the roller coaster we screamed louder and louder, testing the limits of our vocal cords. As the cars chugged up the steep inclines we barely had enough time to catch our breath. Just when we thought we could scream no longer, we were up against the last and most fearsome part of Monstroso . . . the terrifying triple dip.

As the roller coaster neared the top, I could see the expanse of the Fiesta and somehow spotted my mother waving down below. She looked so small. Then the big moment came. Monstroso plunged downward, hurling us to the earth. I shut my eyes as I let out a shriek like never before, for I was certain that my life was over.

"Everybody out!" So that's what God sounds like, I thought.

"Miss, the ride's over," the man said as he cleaned his teeth with a toothpick. "Exit to your left, please."

I opened my eyes to see Emily grinning wildly and my father with his hands in the air. At first I thought he was being held up, then I realized what had happened. He did it. He had finally beaten Monstroso, the Roller Coaster of Death.

Dad and I hugged each other as we jumped up and down. Though we were both proud of our accomplishments, we agreed not to go on Monstroso for another year, or at least until our stomachs had settled.

After bidding farewell to Monstroso and my parents, Emily and I took off. As we ran around the theme park, Emily kept looking over her shoulder. "Do you think Stanford is here?" she asked repeatedly. "Does my hair look okay?"

I scrutinized the ringtoss before moving on to the floating rubber ducks. "I can't believe you still like Stanford knowing that he's just a stupid boy." I realized I sounded hostile. But really, Stanford Wong?

"I still liked you when I thought you were a stupid girl," Emily answered as we turned the corner.

Since Emily and I had reconciled, neither one of us had seen or spoken to Stanford. It was as if he had slithered back under his rock. Although it was neat to have Emily all to myself, it is remotely possible I missed Stanford too. He added another dynamic to our relationship. He made Emily happy, and in the end, that made me happy.

The last time I saw Stanford he was frantically cramming. He had turned in his last book report, but it hadn't been graded yet. All that was left was his final exam. If he passed his English class he would move on to the seventh grade. If he failed, it was sixth grade all over again.

Being a professional, I was determined to help Stanford, even if he did snarl at me every time I corrected him, which was often. As my last task as his tutor, I tossed him a list of what he would need to focus on to pass his test. He took it without looking at me. When I got up to leave, neither of us said a word.

As Emily and I wandered around, I still didn't know Stanford Wong's fate. Emily was convinced he had passed his class. "What I don't understand," she mused, "is why he never apologized. I thought he liked me."

"He does like you, he likes you a lot. But Stanford's afraid you don't think very highly of him," I tried to explain on his behalf. "He thought you liked him because you thought he was really smart."

"Listen," Emily said, stopping so suddenly that the people behind her crashed into us. "What's the big deal about brains anyway? You're supposed to be some genius, but frankly, Millie, and don't take this the wrong way, you're just as dumb as the rest of us. Maybe even dumber, sometimes. As for Stanford, I liked him because he made me laugh, not because he knew what a metaphor was. I also liked that he's not all hung up about the fact that I'm not some skinny supermodel."

I started to analyze what Emily had just said, but stopped myself, figuring that too much analysis was what got me in trouble with Emily in the first place. We started walking again until we came to the Amazing Steve-A-Roni. He was wearing a purple cape and had a turban on his head that looked like one of Maddie's old bath towels.

"Guess your weight for a dollar," he said to me. I guessed his weight to be about 240 pounds.

"Why would I pay you to guess my weight when I already know what it is?" I asked. Before he could reply, Emily pulled me toward the bandstand.

The Rancho Rosetta Rockers were playing "Color My World." My parents like to slow-dance to that song in the living room and I am forever trying to close the curtains lest the neighbors catch a glimpse of them. The last time Dad dipped Mom they both fell down and thought this was terribly funny.

Though I had always associated rock bands with youth, the one on the stage appeared to be made up of middle-aged men in ill-fitting black T-shirts. The drummer looked suspiciously like Dr. Marks, the principal at Star Brite. They all had their eyes closed as they played. I told Emily it was so they didn't have to look at the other band members and be reminded of who they really were.

Emily elbowed me. "Hey!" I cried. She pointed to a group of boys standing off to the side of the stage. They were trying desperately to act cool by slouching and hooking their thumbs though their belt loops.

"I think those boys are looking at us," Emily said, giggling.

I recognized the boys from Stanford's basketball team. They were the same ones who had made fun of me at Monstroso. I started to turn away, but to my horror, Emily smiled at them and waved. I could have killed her. Then the carrot-topped boy nodded and came toward us. Emily straightened up and I stiffened.

"Hello, ladies," he said, smiling.

"Hi," Emily said coyly.

I could not believe she was talking to him.

"Nice song, isn't it?" He looked toward the couples who were slowly making their way around the dance floor.

I waited for him to ask Emily to dance, but to my surprise he turned to me. "May I have this dance?" he asked gallantly.

In the time it took for his words to leave his mouth and meet my ears, my world stood still. Emily let out a little squeal. It was so embarrassing. He looked straight at me and repeated his question. It was a good thing he did because I didn't think I heard him correctly the first time. Our eyes locked and my brain went on overload. *Warning! Warning!* it tried to tell me. Yet another part of me was pleased that he had singled me out.

"Come on, let's dance!" he insisted.

"No, really . . ." I tried to pull myself away. Something about him was familiar.

"Let's dance!" he said, turning to his friends and giving them a thumbs-up.

"Go on," Emily said, grinning. She kept winking at me and I wished she would stop.

I had never danced before. Well, not in public. The sum of my dancing took place in front of the bathroom mirror. I never had occasion to dance with another person, unless you counted when I was a toddler and stood on my father's feet as he leapt around the living room.

Taking my lack of an answer to be a "yes," the boy grabbed my hand and pulled me onto the dance floor. When he slipped his arms around my waist, I stiffened. He was so smooth. I suspected he had done this before. An adolescent Lothario.

"Loosen up," he whispered. He smelled like pine needles or some other familiar household cleaner. As we shuffled around the dance floor, my acid reflux shifted into overload. My hypothalamus went on alert as it received cautionary brain impulses brought on by the presence of an actual boy. I began to hyperventilate, which, I am afraid, he must have mistaken for heavy breathing.

"I feel the same way," he murmured. I could feel his hot breath on my ear. "We don't need this, do we?" he said, as he slipped my briefcase strap off my shoulder.

My briefcase fell to the floor with a dull thud. I felt naked.

More than anything I wanted out of there. Suddenly, I realized why.

"So," he began, "how have you been . . . Mill the Pill?"

I froze. It had been five years since I had last seen Digger, the juvenile delinquent who used to throw food at me. His hair might have faded from red to orange, but my distaste for him hadn't. Ironically, here I was, in a clinch with the very boy who got me expelled from Rancho Rosetta Elementary. I panicked.

"Get away from me," I heard myself saying as I pushed him away. I was not in control of my voice, and my shouting caused the couples around us to stop dancing momentarily.

Digger's eyes narrowed and his face contorted in anger. "You're still just a little nerd," he said loud enough to be heard over the music. "You lost me ten bucks!" I didn't understand. I felt faint as graceful couples pirouetted around us. I was getting dizzy.

Then, to make matters worse, I spotted Stanford heading my way. Why this? Why me? I wished I could just disappear. I shut my eyes.

"Hey, Stan-dude!" Digger said, suddenly smiling. He held up his hand to give Stanford a high five. "What's up?"

"That's what I wanted to ask you," Stanford said, keeping his arms crossed. He looked angry, and I knew he was still mad at me for the Emily misunderstanding.

"Just lost me ten big bucks because this geekazoid here can't dance," Digger said, giving me a look of disdain. "I bet the guys I could get through a whole dance with Miss Smarty-Pants."

Stanford looked at me and I prayed he wouldn't add to my humiliation. To my surprise, he held out his hand. I hesitated, thinking he might pull it away. Maybe the whole thing was a setup. I considered crying.

"It's okay, Millicent," Stanford said. He didn't sound angry. "It's okay."

Something told me it was. I took his hand.

Stanford turned to Digger. "Get lost, loser," he said. "Millie knows how to dance, she just doesn't want to dance with you."

Digger looked shocked. "Hey, Stan the Man, can't you take a joke? It's just that I made a bet and then this nerdball . . ."

"And nothing," Stanford said, cutting him off. Digger appeared to be shrinking as he slunk away. Without looking at me, Stanford put his other hand on my waist and whispered, "Even if you don't know how to dance, pretend you do."

As we marched around the dance floor, I tried to think of something clever and insightful to say. Finally, I hit upon the right words.

"Thank you."

"You're welcome," he said, and added, "and thank you. I passed my English class."

As I was getting the hang of dancing, someone else cut in. "If you ever forget the steps," my father instructed as he twirled me around, "just stand on my feet and enjoy the ride."

Stanford had moved to the side to join Emily. I smiled at them as my father and I covered the dance floor. Stanford looked apologetic and Emily looked happy. As we waltzed past my mother she clutched her teddy bear. She had a strange look of contentment on her face, like she was in a world all her own.

Afterward, my father, Emily, Stanford, and I headed back to Monstroso. I rode six more times, even though I had to ride the last time alone. Both Emily and Stanford said they were done for the day, and Dad pleaded exhaustion. "Back again," the ride operator said. I nodded and handed him a ticket. He waved me through. "This one's on the house," he said.

My last ride was the best. By then I was all screamed out, so I rode in contented silence, with my hands up in the air and a smile on my face, as the Fiesta, my friends and family, and the last days of summer rushed past me in a blur.

Emily spent the night and insisted that Lanford sleep with her along with her favorite beat-up old bear. "I don't think TB minds, do you, Millicent?" she asked as she fluffed up her pillow. As if I would have an opinion about the social lives of stuffed animals.

Lanford is the elephant that Stanford won for Emily at the B-Ball Bushel Throw. He is about twelve times bigger than the bear my dad won for my mom. But then, Stanford made lots more baskets than my father.

The first few times Stanford threw the ball it bounced right out of the bushel. Stanford, who takes unnatural pride in his basketball free-throw skills, was getting frustrated. Then I noticed something funny. I motioned to the man in the booth.

"Want to throw the ball, little girl?" he asked, holding his hand out for a dollar.

"No, I want you to take those out." I pointed to the spare basketballs that sat at the bottom of each bushel.

"No can do," he said, grinning and showing me where his upper teeth were missing.

"I think you can," I told him. I put my hands on my hips to prove how serious I was. "It is clear to me that if there is a ball in the bottom of the bushel it deadens the ball that is thrown. It changes the angle of the refraction of the second ball and causes it to bounce out, making it almost impossible for anyone to win a prize."

The man's eyes narrowed and his smile vanished. "Says you and who else?" he asked. I wondered if he had ever been convicted of a felony or if my murder would be the first.

I looked around. Stanford and Emily were waiting for the man to come back so Stanford could waste more money trying to win a stuffed animal. Just then I spotted a policewoman. I waved to her and yelled, "Good evening, officer!" Turning to the basketball booth man, I said, "Would you mind if I shared my insights with my friend over there?"

"Smart aleck," he snarled as he snatched the money from Stanford's hand and shoved a basketball at him. I glared at the man until he removed the extra balls from the bottom of the bushels.

Every ball Stanford threw made it into the basket and stayed there. I didn't tell him why, only that I thought he was really good at basketball. Stanford gave his giant stuffed elephant to Emily, and they both just stood there beaming at each other for so long I thought I was going to throw up. Emily claims I felt that way because I had gone on Monstroso so many times.

I thought that Dad might feel funny that Stanford won a big stuffed animal and he only won a small one. But nothing could shake his good mood. Right as we were exiting the theme park, Dad stopped us to make an announcement.

"Ah-hem," he said, clearing his throat dramatically. Emily, Mom, and I froze, thinking he was choking on his gum. "You ladies are looking at the new Assistant Manager of Radio Shack!" my father announced, trying hard not to grin.

Mom threw her arms around him and squealed, as Emily and I beamed like proud parents.

Dad's new job starts on Monday and this time it's for real. It is totally perfect. I wish I had thought of it. He spends so much time there, they might as well pay him. Mom is pleased because he finally has a real job, plus he's entitled to a substantial employee discount.

After breakfast this morning we stopped to pick up Maddie. It was a day I had been dreading all summer. Julius, the wooden dragon, greeted us on the front porch. Maddie's asked me to take care of him until she returns.

My grandmother's house was empty except for the suitcases all lined up in the entryway. As Dad tried various configurations to fit them in the trunk, Mom walked around and touched the walls where pictures used to hang.

"C'mon. Let's go!" Maddie said, clapping her hands as she took one last wistful look around. "Don't want to be late for the big event."

Maddie, Emily, and I were squashed in the backseat of the car. Julius sat on my lap since there was no room for him elsewhere. Maddie kept pinching our cheeks and hugging us, but we didn't fuss.

The gym was already full when we arrived. I noticed Stanford sitting near the back bleachers. He waved at me when I saw him and I waved back. Emily turned red and they gave each other almost imperceptible nods that spoke volumes.

"Emily! Millicent, over here!" Alice stood up and motioned us over to the third row. She was wearing a tailored blouse and capris.

Our team finished the season in a respectable third place out of ten. After the rankings were given out we broke off for individual team awards. Julie was named MVP and when Emily accepted the Team Spirit award, Alice leapt up and cheered so loudly that Emily almost fainted from embarrassment. Then Coach Gowin made one final announcement.

"In a unanimous decision, the award for Most Improved Player goes to Millicent Min!"

Most Improved Player? I wasn't sure whether to be flattered or insulted. In the end, I decided to be flattered. Maddie said that anytime your peers single you out, it is an honor. My teammates gave me a standing ovation, and before I could do anything about it, tears flowed freely down my face. What a time for my allergies to act up.

"Hey, Millie," Julie yelled over to me. I thought she was going to make fun of me. Instead, she said, "Nice job."

"See?" my mother whispered as I sat down. She handed me a wad of Kleenex. "You just had to give volleyball a try. Oh," she added, "I almost forgot to tell you, I've signed you up for basketball in the fall."

I was going to protest, but she ran off to the bathroom.

After the awards ceremony, Maddie pulled me aside and fished something out of her big black purse. In her hand rested a small red box. "This is for you, for continued good luck," she said as she ceremoniously placed a green jade pendant on a yellow gold chain around my neck. It complemented Emily's friendship necklace. "I am so proud to see that you're beginning to use your whole self, Millicent. Not just your brain."

When I started to speak, she pressed two fingers to my lips. "Confucius says that you can become part of the moral order of the cosmos once you find your proper place in it. Millicent," Maddie stared deeply into my eyes. "Continue searching out where you belong. Only then will you find happiness."

I wanted to ask her why she felt she had to go to England. Was she searching for her happiness there? Wasn't there anything I could do to make her happy and want to stay here with me? As I opened my mouth to speak, Mom ran up to us. Even if we hurried, there was barely enough time to whisk Maddie to the airport.

Maddie rested her hand on the pendant holding Grandpa's ashes during the entire ride. On her wrist was the beaded bracelet I had made for her. Mom kept looking out the window, and I feared she was going to get sick again. Dad was oblivious to this and wouldn't stop making jokes about driving on the wrong side of the road. Emily was the only one who laughed.

At the airport I hugged Maddie tight and refused to let her go. Emily stood off to the side and for some reason started crying and would not stop, so my mom hugged her while my father looked perplexed.

"Don't fret too much, Millie," Maddie said, taking both my hands in hers.

"Why are you in such a hurry to leave?" I asked.

Maddie gave me another hug. "Millie, the sooner I leave, the sooner I will be back. I'll be home before you know it. I'm just going to Europe, not to Mars." Dad started to make a joke, but Mom shushed him.

Maddie made me promise not to be sad, which is a cruel thing to make a person promise to do, especially when it is nearly impossible. Then she whispered, "I have one more little present for you. I told your mom to give it to you after the plane takes off. Open it when you are alone."

We all waved good-bye as Maddie boarded the plane and then waited until the plane flew away, which was a long time due to the runway being backed up. My mom knew I was depressed, so she said to me, "If we give Maddie a good enough reason, I guarantee you she'll be back."

I started to ask her what she meant, but she got dizzy and had to lie down.

This afternoon Emily and I went shopping, only she didn't buy anything since she is now poor. We had a little ceremony when she cut up her dad's credit card. She had wanted to burn it, but I cautioned her that it might release harmful toxins in the air.

Emily seemed down after she gathered up the pieces of her Visa card and dumped them in the trash. To cheer her up I told her some jokes and actually got her to laugh.

I offered to buy Emily something at the mall since I had my Stanford tutoring cash, plus an extra fifty dollars since he passed his English class with a B-minus. Stanford was quite impressed with himself. If truth be told, he did pull through at the end and do a halfway decent job on his book reports. He had come far, considering where he started at the beginning of summer.

Stanford even gave me a copy of one of his book reports. He was so proud of it.

HOLES, a Book Report by Stanford Wong

Holes is a book written by an author named Louis Sachar. The <u>protagonist</u> is named Stanley and he gets in big trouble for steeling shoes and gets sent to a crummy camp called Camp GreenLake where there is no water. Ha-ha, no water, get it? This is called <u>irony</u>.

Stanley has to dig holes over and over again and he does not like this except he loses weight and that's good because he weighed too much before. He changes in other ways, too, and so do some of the kids around him. Stanley meets a kid named Zero (more irony) and they run away. . . .

It took everything in my power not to laugh as I read it. "Good work," I told him when I was through.

"See, I'm not a complete idiot," Stanford said.

I smiled at him. "No, no, you're pretty bright," I agreed, adding, "for a boy."

As expected, I got an A in my college poetry class. Professor Skylanski says she'll get me a special dispensation so I can take her graduate class when I am a college freshman. That is, if I go to Rogers College. I'm thinking Ivy League, but Mom says that I still have another year and that "a lot can happen in a year." I think she is trying to prepare me for the inevitable.

At the mall Emily and I stopped for an ice cream, my treat. I was feeling melancholy and she sensed it immediately. Friends are like that. You don't even have to talk, they just know how you are feeling.

"What?" she asked.

"I'm really going to miss you," I told her.

"Why, where are you going?" She had gotten a double scoop of strawberry and it was dripping.

"I'm not going anywhere, it's you who's going away."

"I'm not going anywhere either."

"You're starting school tomorrow and you have your whole life in front of you." My double Dutch chocolate ice cream tasted bland.

"Gawd, Millicent, you're so dramatic," Emily said, laughing.

"Well, it's true," I said, trying not to sound hurt.

"Silly Millie, we'll always be best friends."

"I hope so."

With Emily, everything is so simple. But I know better. She's practically going steady with Stanford. And when school begins, it is certain that she will make new friends. Then where will I be? A high school senior with only my Math Bowl National Championship and valedictorian speech to look forward to.

I feel so lonely.

I couldn't sleep last night. So I slipped out of the house and up into my tree. The air was dry and a warm wind stirred up the leaves. Dogs were barking in the distance and I saw Max running down the street wearing a Superman cape. His parents ran behind him as if in slow motion, their bathrobes flapping as they shouted out his name.

From my vantage point I could see the constellations. I trained my grandfather's telescope toward the stars as they winked at me reassuringly. The night was beautiful.

"What do you see up there?"

"Grandpa?" I asked.

It was my father, standing at the base of the tree in his pajamas and slippers. He shined a flashlight in my face. I shielded my eyes. "Come on up, Dad," I said.

"Really?" he asked. "You mean that?" He put down the flashlight. The only other time he had been in my tree was when we first built the shelves several years ago. After that, it went unspoken that it was my private place.

Awkwardly, my father climbed the tree and took my hand as I tried to steady him. There was little room for both of us, but neither of us minded. We watched as Max's parents carried him kicking and yelling back into their house.

"I'll bet you've seen a lot of interesting things from up here," Dad said, staring off into the sky. We were both silent for a while. Then he asked, "Do you miss Maddie?"

"Yes," I answered, wondering how he knew. I missed her so much and she had only been gone a couple days.

"Me too," he said, sounding surprised. "But she'll be back and in our hair again before we know it."

The door creaked open slowly and Mom came out. Dad and I held our breath so she would not hear us. She lifted her arms up like a ballerina. Then she twirled around, threw some leaves into the air, and retreated back into the house. We both resumed breathing.

"What was that all about?" I asked.

"I don't really understand most of what your mother does," my father mused. "I just know that she loves us, and that's enough for me. Come on, let's go back inside before she notices we're missing and starts to worry. You need to try to get some sleep. You start your senior year of high school tomorrow."

"Wait." I tugged on his pajama top. I was quiet for a moment, then said, "Everybody's leaving me, Dad."

"I won't ever leave you, Millicent."

"And I won't leave you either," I promised.

"That's a nice thought. But someday you will, when you grow up. That's what kids are supposed to do. Just don't be in such a hurry, okay?"

"Dad," I asked as we walked toward the house. "Next weekend, would you teach me how to throw a Frisbee?"

He stopped and turned toward me. "Are you just asking to make me feel better?"

"No, I really want to." The funny thing was, I really did.

"Well, in that case, I really want to, too," he said. Even though it was dark, I could see that he was smiling. He gave me a big bear hug. After a few minutes I worried I might suffocate.

"You can let go now," I gasped.

"What if I'm not ready to let go?"

"Time for bed, Dad," I said, catching my breath. I hesitated and then whispered, "Mom's really sick, isn't she?"

"Is that what you think?" He sounded surprised.

"I know it."

His face grew pensive and he opened his mouth as if to say something, but stopped himself. "Go on into your room. I'll get Mom, she has something to tell you. We were going to wait. The doctor said it would be best not to tell anyone for another two weeks, just in case . . . But under the circumstances . . . well, I'll get your mother."

While I waited, I moved Julius around my room, hoping to find a suitable place for him. Finally I put him next to the window. The moon cast his shadow against the wall. As I sat on my bed and hugged my knees, I could hear my parents murmuring in the hallway. It was comforting and disconcerting at the same time. When my mom finally came in I threw my arms around her and choked back tears. "I knew it, I knew it," I sobbed. "I was right, wasn't I?"

"Millie," she said softly, gently. "Calm down."

"Are you going to die? Just tell me. I have to know."

She looked at me and shook her head. Then she began to cry too, and for the first time I got really, really scared. She took my hands in hers. "Sweetheart," she said, not bothering to dry her tears, "I'm not going to die, I'm going to have a baby."

I was stunned. I felt like all the air had been sucked out of me, but in a good way. "A baby?" I said, startled. "How can that be?"

"Well, Millicent," my mother began as she plucked a leaf from her hair. "When a man and a woman . . ."

"I know that," I said. "I just mean . . . I mean, you're going to live?"

Mom laughed. I love to hear her laugh, she has a great infectious laugh. "It is certainly my plan to live a good long life with my husband and two children and numerous grandchildren."

I was giddy. "Does that mean I'm going to be a big sister?"

My mother smiled widely. "Yes, that's usually how it works."

It was too much to comprehend. First, my mother wasn't going to die, and second, I was going to be a sister. Me, a big sister.

"Does Dad know about this?" I asked.

Mom burst out laughing. "I'm fairly certain he does."

I knew I sounded like a blubbering idiot, but I couldn't help it, I was so happy. I couldn't wait to tell Emily.

When I was finally alone, I reached under my pillow and pulled out Chow Lee Low. Maddie had left me a little red cable knit sweater and a note that read:

> Dearest Millie,
>   I know you don't know where Chow Lee Low ran off to. But if he does come home, here is a new sweater for him so he does not catch cold.
>
>   Love always,
>   Your Maddie

When I took Chow Lee Low from Maddie's Chinese chest, I never meant to keep him. I was planning to give him back, but just never got around to it. I would never even consider sleeping with a stuffed animal. Still, there is something remotely comforting about having Chow Lee Low by my side.

Maybe when my sister/brother is born, I will give Chow Lee Low to the baby. Or maybe back to Mom, or to Maddie. Or maybe I'll just keep him after all. I don't know. Given the day's events, and the whole summer for that matter, I am too happy and sad and tired to even think.

THE TOWER OF LONDON, LONDON, ENGLAND

Millicent,
Heard the great news!
Back in time to welcome my
new grandchild (and to hug my
old one).

Love,
Maddie

P.S. The Queen sends her regards.

MILLICENT L. MIN
521 RIDGESIDE DRIVE
RANCHO ROSETTA, CA
92219

RF

DATE DUE

JAN 0 3 2006			
OCT 2 2 2007			